DCC8
1/1/12
THY 1/14
3/9/14
ORT 9/15

PETERBOROUGH LIBRARIES

This book is to be returned on or before the latest date shown above, but may be renewed up to three times if the book is not in demand. Ask at your local library for details.

Please note that charges are made on overdue books

60000 0000 46852

"I'm torn between throttling you and kissing you."

His throat went dry the second the words left his mouth.

Their gazes locked again, and what he saw on her face stole his breath. She looked as she did the night in his hotel room. Cheeks flushed to a rosy pink. Lips slightly parted. The memory of how soft those lips felt pressed against his own had him moving closer, too, despite every warning bell going off in his head.

It was hard to breathe. Or think. Yeah, he really wasn't thinking as his head dipped ever so slightly. His body went tighter than a drum, taut with anticipation.

His pulse raced.

Her eyes glimmered with reluctant heat.

Their heads moved closer, their lips mere inches away. The scent of her hair drifted into his nostrils, sweet and feminine and so very addictive. He breathed her in, drowning in the scent, while his body hummed eagerly and his mouth tingled with the need to taste her.

So he did.

Dear Reader,

Falling in love with your kidnapper… I'll be honest—this might be the toughest premise I've ever had to work with. Then again, I always love a good challenge, and I think it's sometimes fun and exciting to step out of your comfort zone and push the boundaries.

The hero of this story, Deacon Holt, believes there is darkness inside of him. So what better way to show him the light than to pair him with the beautiful, idealistic Lana Kelley, a woman who sees beauty in everything? Redemption stories have always been a favorite of mine, and I hope you enjoy Deacon and his path to redemption!

I'm always happy to hear from readers, so visit my website, www.ellekennedy.com, and drop me a line.

Happy reading!

Elle Kennedy

Missing Mother-To-Be

ELLE KENNEDY

First published in Great Britain 2012
by Mills & Boon, an imprint of Harlequin (UK) Limited.
Large Print edition 2012
Harlequin (UK) Limited,
Eton House, 18-24 Paradise Road,
Richmond, Surrey TW9 1SR

© Harlequin Books S.A. 2011

Special thanks and acknowledgment to Elle Kennedy for her contribution to *The Kelley Legacy* miniseries.

ISBN: 978 0 263 23007 9

Printed and bound in Great Britain
by CPI Antony Rowe, Chippenham, Wiltshire

ELLE KENNEDY

A RITA® Award-nominated author, Elle Kennedy grew up in the suburbs of Toronto, Ontario, and holds a B.A. in English from York University. From an early age, she knew she wanted to be a writer, and actively began pursuing that dream when she was a teenager. She loves strong heroines and sexy alpha heroes, and just enough heat and danger to keep things interesting.

Elle loves to hear from her readers. Visit her website, www.ellekennedy.com, for the latest news or to send her a note.

To Marie, Beth, Gail, Carla and Cindy—
I'm honored to be part of a miniseries
with such talented and fabulous authors!

Prologue

Don't worry, kiddo. There's nothing you can do here.

Sinking her teeth into her bottom lip, Lana Kelley stared at the timeless masterpiece in front of her, the white marble's graceful curves bringing only a fraction of the soothing serenity art normally gave her. Her older brother's words continued to run through her mind. Why was it that when someone told you not to worry it only made you worry more?

Ever since her phone call with Dylan, she'd been debating whether to hop on a plane back to the States or to take her brother's advice and stay put. The inner debate had eventually brought her here, to this surprisingly deserted wing of the Louvre, which housed the celebrated Venus de Milo. Throughout her entire life, she'd felt most at peace in a museum. It was as if the magnificent works of art possessed the ability to calm her, help clear her mind so she could make sense of the chaos out in the real world.

And her world, more often than not, was definitely chaotic. The youngest daughter of a United States senator and an oil heiress, Lana had spent most of her twenty-four years in the public eye, a position she hadn't always enjoyed. She preferred holing up in the spacious studio her dad had set up for her in their California mansion, running her fingers over warm dusty clay. This past year, though, had been welcomingly *un*chaotic. Living in Florence, working on her master's degree in art history—for once, she'd been able to live her life out of the public eye.

Her father, on the other hand, seemed completely incapable of discretion.

Senator's Dirty Little Secret.

The newspaper headline she'd come across earlier today flashed across her mind, bringing a pretzel of pain to her belly. What had her father been *thinking?* And if the news of his infidelities had reached Paris, where she was spending her summer vacation, she could just imagine how bad things were back home.

Dylan had sounded so disgusted with their dad. Hardly a surprise. Growing up, she'd witnessed her father's tumultuous relationship with her five older brothers, but Lana had been fortunate enough to experience a different side of Hank Kelley. She was the apple of her dad's eye, and she loved him deeply, despite his spoiled and reckless nature.

But she loved her mother, too, and her heart ached at the thought of what Mom must be going through right now. Her stomach burned with grief and regret. She wished she were home to support her mother, and heck, even her dad, who must be horribly embarrassed and riddled with guilt over the pain he'd caused. But Dylan had urged her to go back to Florence for the new term and focus on her studies.

"We're closing in thirty minutes, mademoiselle." The hesitant voice of the armed guard manning the gallery door drew her from her thoughts.

Lana lifted her head, startled. She'd heard a staff member announce that the museum would be closing in an hour—hadn't that been only a couple of minutes ago? She glanced at her silver Cartier watch and frowned. No, the guard was right. The announcement had been a while ago. She must have spaced out again.

"I'll be leaving shortly," she assured the guard. "I lost track of time."

She noticed his gaze flit over the watch circling her wrist, as if he couldn't believe she could lose track of time while wearing such an expensive watch. Stifling a sigh, Lana let the sleeve of her red wool sweater slide down to hide the watch's diamond-studded face. It had been a gift from her father, and though she hated extravagant shows of wealth, she felt guilty when she didn't wear the darn thing. Almost as if Hank Kelley could sense, from another continent no less, the moment she took the watch off her wrist.

"I'm sure the director would be inclined to keep the exhibit open should you require more time to peruse the pieces, Ms. Kelley," the tall man hedged in his thick French accent.

Another sigh rose up her chest. She swallowed that one down, too. Of course. She should've known the director would inform the guards of her identity. Louis Dupont was an old acquaintance of her mother's, and he always treated Lana like a princess when she came to visit.

"That won't be necessary," she said quickly. "I have somewhere to be anyway."

Yet instead of gathering her purse and the small sketchbook she'd brought with her, her gaze drifted back to the beautiful statue in front of her. Not yet. She didn't want to go yet, not when her nerves were still coiled in tense knots.

"The museum is closing in thirty minutes."

Frowning, Lana glanced at the guard, wondering why he felt the need to remind her of something he'd uttered seconds ago, but then she noticed the warning wasn't directed at her. A tall man in black wool trousers and a hunter-green sweater stood near the large arched doorway off to her left, and it was him the guard had spoken to.

She hadn't noticed anyone else in the quiet, spacious room, and the sight of the ruggedly handsome stranger immediately sparked her interest. He was in his mid to late thirties, with brown hair cut in a short, military-like style, and an unbelievably gorgeous face. High cheekbones, a strong jaw and straight aristocratic nose, sensual lips—very much like the classically handsome, chiseled features of the statues gracing the gallery. Yet it wasn't just his looks that captured her attention. There was something simmering below his perfectly sculpted surface. Something dark and powerful and very, very sexy.

The man nodded in response to the guard's notification, but made no move to leave. Rather, he stepped closer to the Venus de Milo, his hazel eyes fixed on the statue as the guard edged back to the door.

"She's beautiful, huh?" The question slipped out of Lana's mouth before she could stop it. She didn't usually strike up conversations with strangers, but the look in the man's eyes was so very...*haunting.*

He turned slightly, not even blinking. "Yes. She is."

"I always imagine her whole, with long graceful arms, adorned with jewels. We think she's a beauty now, but can you imagine how much more beautiful she'd be?" Lana felt her cheeks grow warm as the random and somewhat pretentious remark passed through her lips. She tended to get caught up when surrounded by art, and she suddenly experienced a pang of embarrassment, unleashing an art lecture on a total stranger.

But to her surprise, his features softened. Those hazel eyes shone with intensity as he locked his gaze with hers. "Divine beauty," he said simply.

His husky voice made her heart skip a beat. It was deep, rough, like a gruff purr.

"Exactly," she murmured. When he didn't respond, she awkwardly clasped her hands together in her lap. "I love it here," she found herself blurting. "Just looking at all these pieces makes me feel…at peace. Does that happen to you?"

The stranger's eyes never left hers. "Yes. It does."

"It's as though all the problems in the world just fade away," she went on, a faraway note entering her voice. "At least that's what usually happens. Right now, I can't stop thinking about

everything going on back home. My family…
God, what a mess."

The man seemed to hesitate for a moment, as
if debating whether or not to get the heck out of
there before she burst into tears or something.
Lana didn't blame him. What was she thinking,
dumping her problems on a stranger?

"I'm sorry." She laughed in discomfort. "I
don't normally burden people I don't know with
my issues."

"It's not a burden." His voice came out rough.
"Did something happen back home?"

She nodded numbly. "Yeah. Yeah, something
happened. And I want so badly to fly back and
help, but my brother says there's nothing I can
do."

"He's probably right." Her stranger shrugged.
"I've learned it's often better to let others clean
up their own messes."

"Maybe." Lana rested her hands on her knees.
"I just hate feeling powerless."

A wry half smile lifted his mouth. "As does most of the world."

She smiled back. "You're right. Nobody likes it, do they?" Impulsively, she got to her feet and stuck out her hand. "I'm Lana."

Another beat of hesitation, and then he slowly reached out and shook her hand, oddly gentle. Somehow she didn't suspect *gentleness* was a word you'd normally associate with this man. Now that she was standing up, she realized exactly how big he was. Well over six feet, and the muscles rippling beneath his green sweater looked rock-hard.

A thrill shot through her body, which surprised her. This had never happened to her before, such a quick, visceral attraction, the almost eerie awareness of this man as *male*. She didn't have much experience in the attraction department, aside from high-school crushes and that one disastrous relationship when she was doing her undergrad.

"Deacon."

That timber-rough voice jolted her from her thoughts. Deacon. She tilted her head to meet his eyes again. Yes, he looked like a Deacon. It was a strong name, very fitting for this man who just radiated strength.

"Deacon," she echoed, a mere whisper.

His hazel eyes went darker, burning with something unidentifiable. As if the sound of his name on her lips had elicited something inside him.

"You're an American," she added, a statement, not a question. His accent wasn't Parisian. Not European, either.

"I grew up in Boston," he confirmed, and then his lips tightened shut, as if the revelation displeased him.

"East coast," she said, a teasing note to her voice. "I'm from the west. Just a spoiled little rich girl from Beverly Hills."

Those sensual lips relaxed, lifting slightly. "Somehow I don't think the word *spoiled* applies to you."

She offered another smile. "But maybe I am. Maybe I'm spoiled rotten."

Deacon shook his head. "No. Money doesn't interest you." His gaze slid down to her fancy watch. "I think you would even give that watch to a beggar on the street if you didn't have change."

Surprise jolted through her. "You sound very certain of that."

"Am I wrong?"

"No," she admitted. "I'm not interested in material things. And I *would* give this darn watch away, if it hadn't been a gift."

Deacon had that look about him, the smug one of a man who'd totally pegged her. "I bet you even gave your trust fund to charity, didn't you, Lana?"

Her lips twitched. Yep, he had her pegged. "The day I turned twenty-one," she confirmed. She neglected to mention that her irate father had promptly deposited the same amount back into her account. She didn't have the heart to give the second trust away; spoiling her gave her father such silly pleasure.

"So…" Deacon cocked his head thoughtfully. "If money doesn't interest you, then what does?"

His question gave her pause. "Family," she replied. "And sculpting. I could never give up my art."

"Ah, you yearn to make the world a more beautiful place." There was a slight edge to his tone.

"Why not?" She shrugged carelessly. "There's so much ugliness in the world these days. What's wrong with wanting to replace some of it with beauty?"

"An idealist. I should have known."

She studied his face. "You don't believe in the power of beauty?"

Deacon went quiet. His hazel eyes locked with hers once more, and there it was again, that intense ripple of energy beneath his surface. Only this time it was accompanied by heat. Heavy, sizzling heat that seemed to hang in the air, hovering over them, crackling between them.

"Yes," he finally said, his voice thick. "I believe in the power of beauty."

His gaze swept across her body, resting on her breasts, her hips, and then moving back to her face. Her heart jumped again. And her breasts were suddenly achy, her nipples tingling against her bra. What *was* this? Lust at first sight? No, she didn't lust over strange men. She was far too levelheaded for primitive urges.

And yet, when she opened her mouth, the words that slid out proved that maybe she was far lustier than she'd ever imagined. "Would you…like to have a drink with me?"

Surprised flickered on his handsome face. He took a step back, as if he wanted to flee. But he didn't. Instead, his massive chest rose as he drew in a breath, and then one husky word echoed in the empty gallery.

"Yes."

Chapter 1

Two weeks later

Were there right and wrong ways to pee on a stick? Lana stared down at the plastic cylinder between her trembling fingers, the two pink lines as clear as a billboard in Times Square. She must be doing something wrong. This was the fourth test she'd taken in two days. Eight pink lines. It *had* to be a mistake.

"Attention tous les passagers," a loud voice blared in French through the PA. The voice informed her that the train to Florence was now boarding, prompting Lana to leave the bathroom stall.

Her shaky legs carried her to the trash can near the door, where she tossed the pregnancy test before turning to examine her reflection in the mirror. Her blond hair was pulled back in a low ponytail, her face was makeup-free and there were dark smudges under her eyes. She looked tired.

Didn't look pregnant, though.

Her gaze slid down to her abdomen, which was flat beneath her red V-neck tee. And her snug black capris fitted the same as always, comfortably circling her waist

She lifted her head, suddenly feeling silly. Of course she wouldn't be showing yet. It had only been two weeks. Two weeks since that crazy, wonderful night with Deacon.

Quickly washing her hands, she dried them with a paper towel then dropped it in the trash, effectively covering the pregnancy test that seemed to glare accusingly up at her.

She drew in a calming breath. Okay. Okay, this wasn't the end of the world. She was pregnant, not deathly ill. She would get on the train, go back to her apartment in Florence and figure things out.

How will you find him? a desperate little voice demanded.

Lana left the bathroom, tugging on the handle of her sleek black suitcase and rolling it behind her. The distressed plea in her mind was hard to ignore. How *would* she find him? She'd gone back to his hotel last night, after the first two tests had shown positive, but the clerk in the lobby informed her that Mr. Holt had checked out. Holt. At least she got a last name out of that visit.

She dodged a woman dragging an enormous suitcase, and continued down the terminal. The station was busy, filled with evening travelers rushing up and down the tiled floor. People chattered on in French, Italian and a smattering of other languages, completely oblivious to Lana's inner turmoil.

How on earth would she track down Deacon?

The hotel didn't have a forwarding address for him, and a quick Google search on her laptop had come up with nothing. She didn't even know what he did for a living, for Pete's sake. A businessman, he'd said. Great. *So* much to go on there.

"May I help you with your suitcase?" a purser asked in French as Lana approached the track.

"Merci, oui," she murmured.

The thin man picked up her suitcase then helped her onto the train. A loud whistle pierced the air. Travelers were bounding down the platform, boarding at the last minute, while the PA crackled again to announce the train's departure.

A pretty woman with shiny brown hair escorted Lana to her compartment. It was a private sleeper car, and she'd already arranged for a wake-up call for tomorrow morning, when she'd need to take the connecting train in Milan. The cabin was cozy and comfortable, but Lana doubted she'd get any sleep. Probably just sit in silence for the next nine hours and try not to cry.

God, what kind of mess had she found herself in?

She sank down on the plush bench and promptly buried her face in her hands.

"Is everything all right, mademoiselle?" the stewardess asked hesitantly.

Lana lifted her head. "Everything is fine," she managed. "I'm just tired."

The woman stored Lana's suitcase on the overhead rack and edged to the door. "I will let you rest then. Enjoy the trip."

Lana muttered a thank-you, then let out a breath as the door of the compartment closed and she was alone.

Alone.

Oh, God, she'd have to raise this baby by herself.

The moment the thought slid into her mind, a surprising sense of calm settled over her. Ever since she'd taken those tests, she hadn't allowed herself to think about what she planned to do with the baby. She was twenty-four years old, unmarried, still being supported by her parents to supplement the small income she made selling her sculptures. Having a child hadn't been in her foreseeable future.

But circumstances had changed. She was pregnant. And no matter how unexpected this development, she knew she would keep the baby.

Her hand covered her stomach, a rush of startling joy sweeping through her as she imagined the tiny life growing inside her. A baby. *Her* baby.

And Deacon's...

The joy faded into frustration. Yes, this was Deacon's child, too. And he had no clue.

She had to find a way to contact him. Sure, he probably wouldn't be thrilled about the news. For all she knew, he'd turn on his heel and march away without a backward glance, not wanting anything to do with this child. The notion brought a spark of pain and anger to her gut, but she wasn't naive enough to dwell on the anger. She and Deacon were strangers. Two strangers who'd met one night and found comfort and magic in each other's arms.

She couldn't expect him to welcome the idea of fatherhood with open arms. She wouldn't even blame him if he didn't. But he still had a right to know. Lana wouldn't be able to live with herself knowing she'd kept something as important as a *child* from the man.

She had to track him down. So what if he didn't seem to want to be found? So what if it would be difficult? She was Lana Kelley, after all. Her shoulders straightened in determination. When she reached Florence, she'd call a private investigator and hire him to find Deacon. And then she'd sit down and figure out what to do about this last year of school. She could probably finish out the winter semester, but she wanted to be in the States when the baby was born. She wanted her family to—

Her family.

Lana felt all the color drain from her face. "They're going to kill me," she mumbled to herself.

She pictured her brothers' faces when they heard the news and suddenly grew nauseous. Her parents might understand, maybe even support her. They might have their own problems at the moment, but everything would be straightened out eventually. Once that happened, she knew her mom and dad would help her.

Her brothers, on the other hand…

Dylan and Cole would be furious. Jake might be supportive, if he ever returned from his mysterious undercover assignment that had taken him away from them for two years now. Chase probably wouldn't care—he'd washed his hands of the family years ago. And Jim, well, he'd probably hunt Deacon down and rip his throat out.

A hysterical laugh bubbled in her throat. At least then she'd be able to tell Deacon the news.

Reaching for the black leather purse she'd set down beside her, Lana fumbled inside it until she found her cell phone. The train was already tearing down the tracks, heading for Florence, but she couldn't wait until she got there. She had to talk to someone. Anyone. She needed some moral support badly.

She scrolled through her contact list, hesitating on her mother's number. No, she finally decided. Mom had her own worries right now. Regret gathered in Lana's belly. Darn it. She hated adding any more stress on her mother's already over-full plate.

Caitlin O'Donahue's number was what she dialed instead. Lana considered Caitlin family, the older sister she'd never had, not to mention her very best friend. Caitlin had babysat Lana when they were growing up, and over the years had become her closest confidante.

"Hey, you've reached Caitlin. Leave a message and I'll get back to you," her friend's voice chirped.

Lana hung up in frustration, not bothering to leave a message. *I got knocked up after a one-night-stand* wasn't something you wanted to say over voice mail.

She shoved the phone in her bag and leaned her head back. What a mess. Why had Deacon checked out of his hotel so abruptly?

And why couldn't she get him out of her head?

The memory of their night together floated into her mind like a balmy summer breeze. Her body grew hot, tight and achy, as she remembered the feel of his strong arms wrapped around her.

"You're stunning," he'd whispered into her neck. And then he'd looked at her with those sexy hazel eyes, as if he'd truly never known beauty until that night.

The entire encounter was still so surreal. The tangy flavor of the red wine they'd sipped. His warm breath, heating her skin. His lips, kissing their way along her collarbone, her jaw, finally pressing against her mouth.

Her skin broke out in shivers. God, those kisses. Soft and romantic, teasing, fleeting and then hot and passionate, as the heat between them exploded in a raging fire that had left her utterly sated.

"This isn't a good idea," he'd murmured between kisses, uncertainty flickering on his handsome face. "We're strangers."

Yes, they were. Two strangers who'd met in a museum, shared a few glasses of wine in a hotel room and wound up needy and naked in bed.

It had been the best night of her life.

Lana's gaze dropped to her flat abdomen. Maybe the worst, too, yet she couldn't quite bring herself to regret the result of their passion. A baby. God, a *baby*.

Those two words continued to echo through her mind, and she clung to them. The tiny life growing inside her was the only thing keeping her grounded at the moment. The only reason she hadn't gone into a total panic and started roaming the streets of Paris in search of

Deacon. She needed to be strong for this child. She needed to love it and protect it.

Protect it, she repeated in her mind, as her eyelids became heavy. She wasn't sure why the slightly ominous notion rolled inside her head, but she clung to that, too, as sleep slowly crept in.

She wasn't sure how long she slept, but when her eyes snapped open a while later, it was pitch black inside the cabin, and all she saw out the window was darkness. The train was still moving, the wheels making a metallic click-clack sound as they sped along the rails.

Lana glanced at her watch and saw it was almost five in the morning, a half-hour before her scheduled wake-up call. Rubbing her tired eyes, she stood up and went to the small sink in the corner of the cabin, where she brushed her teeth and washed her face. Then she sat down again, wide awake as she waited for the train to reach Milan.

The wake-up knock sounded from the door

thirty minutes later, and when the train's wheels finally screeched to a halt, Lana was more than ready to get off and board the connecting train to Florence. She should've just hopped a flight, it would've gotten her home a lot sooner, but she'd always thought traveling through Europe by train was charming.

Now she just found it time-consuming.

She was at the door of the cabin when the train came to a creaky stop, so when the second knock came, she already had her hand on the door handle.

"I'm all ready," she said as she opened the door. "My suitcase is—"

Her words halted in her throat as she laid eyes on two very large, very menacing-looking men. The taller of the two had a shaved head and a lethal jagged scar along his left cheekbone. The second man was shorter, but not lacking in muscle. He had the shoulders of a linebacker, dark skin the color of rich chocolate and a pair of chilly brown eyes.

There was a third man behind them, but he had his back turned, as if he were scouting the narrow corridor of the train.

A lookout.

The thought flew into her head swiftly, making her hands grow cold. "Can I help you?" she asked cautiously.

Scar Cheek seemed to be smirking, though his lips were snapped together in a rigid line. It was Cold Eyes who responded to her question. "You're going to need to come with us."

He spoke in English, and the harsh look on his face brooked no argument.

Lana argued. "I'm sorry, you must have me mistaken for someone else. I'm not—"

Her sentence died with a squeak. Cold Eyes had just shifted the bottom of his long black trench coat, revealing the sleek gun in his right hand.

"Listen to me, and listen carefully," he said, his voice eerily soft. "You are going to follow us off this train like a good little girl. If you scream,

I'll put a bullet between your eyes. If you try to run, I'll put one in your leg. Understood?"

She nodded dazedly, terror circling her spine like icy fingers. What the hell was going on? Her first thought was that this might be a terrorist attack, that the train had been hijacked, but the corridor remained as silent as a church. No frightened screams, no terrified whimpers.

These men…

They were here for *her.*

"Now pick up your suitcase," Cold Eyes ordered, his hand still resting on the butt of his weapon.

As her heart thudded like a bass drum, Lana numbly bent down to grab the handle of her suitcase. Her fingers shook so wildly she could barely get a grip on the bag. Finally, she did, heaving it off the ground.

"Good girl," Cold Eyes said with mock encouragement. "Now follow us. And remember what I told you."

Her feet felt cold and heavy, but she forced

them to move. The two men immediately flanked her, keeping her sandwiched between them like bodyguards. The third man she'd noticed walked in front of them. He wore a long black coat like his fellow henchmen, and all she saw of him was a head of dark, close-cropped hair and broad shoulders. But something about his gait, those confident but wary strides…it was very familiar.

Alarm skittered through her as they walked. Cabin doors were beginning to open, bleary-eyed passengers stepping out into the corridor ready to disembark. Lana felt a sudden spike of adrenaline. There were people around. Cold Eyes might be hiding his gun underneath his big coat, but no way would he pull that thing out in front of all of these people.

Would he?

Her palms went damp, sweat coating the handle of her suitcase. Should she call their bluff? Scream like a banshee? They wouldn't shoot her with so many eyewitnesses. They wouldn't—

"Don't even think about it," Cold Eyes murmured, glancing at her with a pleasant smile.

"You won't do it," she murmured back, her voice shaking like a leaf in a hurricane. "You won't shoot me with all these people around."

"Maybe not," he replied casually. "But one phone call and your mother dies."

Panic slammed into her. Mom? No, he was bluffing. Her mother was staying with an old girlfriend at Martha's Vineyard, according to her brother Dylan. No way could these men know that.

"A friend of mine is staring through the scope of a rifle as we speak, and your mother's pretty little face is in his sights. The Vineyard is lovely this time of year, don't you think?"

Her pulse shrieked between her eyes. Oh, God. They *did* know where her mom was. She forced herself to stay calm. Okay, this didn't mean anything. Just because they knew her mom's location didn't mean some sniper was actually situated there. Cold Eyes could still be bluffing, but…if he wasn't… Lord, if he wasn't, she wasn't about to endanger her mother's life by causing a scene.

Better to get off the train with these men. Maybe she could lose them in the terminal. Maybe—

The barrel of a gun jammed into her side. "Keep walking." Scar Cheek, this time, and he had a deep rumble of a voice. He had a gun, too, and was now using it to make sure she kept to the rapid pace they'd set for her.

They neared the door. Lana's gaze darted around like that of a scared rabbit, trying to find a way out of this, a person whose eye she could catch. But the other passengers were filing off the train, chatting obliviously to one another, as the purser helped them onto the platform.

The man ahead of them got off first. Again, she experienced a weird sense of familiarity. She *knew* him. The hard set of the shoulders, the almost militarily precise walk. It reminded her of her brother Jim, who was a trained Special

Forces operative. He moved with that same predatory grace.

Lana was suddenly heaved down the steps, her suitcase thudding onto the floor of the train platform. Cold Eyes stood directly beside her, his brown eyes dark with irritation and impatience. "Faster," he ordered. "And put a smile on your damn face."

A smile? She was seconds away from bursting into tears. Hot moisture painfully pricked her eyelids and her throat was so tight she could barely draw in a breath. But then she remembered the gun tucked in his coat, and forced her lips to cooperate. She tugged up the corners of her mouth, trying to look happy, to pretend that she wasn't being taken hostage by three fierce-looking thugs.

The smile didn't hold, though. It lasted all of three seconds, until the third man whose face she still hadn't seen finally turned around.

A shocked gasp flew out of her throat.

Oh, *God*.

It was Deacon! Deacon, standing right there on the platform, the hem of his trench coat blowing around from the brisk wind in the station.

Their eyes locked. For one brief second, hope shot up her chest, warming her heart. He was here. He was going to save her. He was—

"Keep walking," Deacon snapped, and all the hope in her body fizzled like a wet candle.

She felt pressure against her hip. Realized Scar Cheek was pressing his gun into her back. Fear spiraled through her. Fear and amazement and pure and utter shock.

Deacon. Was here. He was here, with two other men. With guns.

Oh, God, she was being kidnapped by the father of her baby.

Chapter 2

Deacon Holt was not a religious man. Never had been, probably never would be. Yet at that moment, as he stared into Lana Kelley's bottomless blue eyes, he found himself praying.

Praying that she'd keep her mouth shut.

If she said his name, or let on that they'd slept together, they'd both be screwed. Le Clair wouldn't think twice about yanking Deacon's ass off this assignment, and if that happened, Lana Kelley would be utterly alone. Defenseless.

Dead.

Deacon forced the troubling thought from his head and kept walking. A quick backward

glance and he confirmed that the flood of familiarity was still swimming on Lana's gorgeous
face. She knew exactly who he was.

Well, no kidding. They'd gone to bed with
each other, of course she wouldn't forget that.

Frustration gathered in his gut, making his in-
testines burn. Damn it. Why, *why* had he slept
with her? He'd always prided himself on pos-
sessing incredible control, yet one look at Lana
Kelley's flawless features and slender fragile
body, and he'd been a goner. He was supposed
to be tailing her, monitoring her movements
until Le Clair got word from his bosses that the
mission was a go. Instead, he'd fallen into bed
with the woman, unable to steel himself against
her soft, melodic voice and big blue eyes.

At least Le Clair didn't suspect anything. After
Lana left his hotel room that night, Deacon had
reported in, informing his boss that inadver-
tent contact had been made. Le Clair promptly
pulled him off tailing rotation, and Deacon had
spent the past two weeks alternating between

the urge to kick himself and the need to see Lana Kelley again.

Somehow, the woman had gotten under his skin. Big-time.

And yet you're kidnapping her, said the mocking voice in his head.

Deacon didn't allow himself to dwell on the sliver of guilt that pricked his skin. This was business. He might have messed up and screwed the target, but he wasn't about to screw himself. His work as a mercenary was all he had. He'd been forced to fend for himself since he was fifteen years old, making money by whatever means necessary. And he hadn't gotten to this point by distracting himself with foolish human emotions like guilt. Emotions, frankly, were a waste of time, and he forced himself to remember that as he led the group toward the exit of the station.

Behind him, Charlie and Tango were practically dragging Lana, urging her in hard tones to keep walking. Deacon had never worked with the two men before. Didn't even know their real names. Le Clair assigned each team member names from the military alphabet, corresponding to the letters of their first name. So Charlie and Tango could be Carl and Tom, or Chris and Tim, for all Deacon knew. But they were pros, that much was evident. They'd handled Lana Kelley with supreme efficiency back on that train.

Deacon might even have been impressed by their professionalism, if he hadn't been battling the ridiculous urge to take Lana into his arms and carry her off the train to safety.

What the hell was the matter with him?

Focus. You're on a job.

Deacon drew in a calming breath. Okay. He had to quit remembering the way Lana Kelley looked naked—as mind-blowing as the image was—and treat her as he did any other target. Faceless. Nameless. A means to an end. And in this case, the end was a staggering amount of money. Whoever had hired Le Clair was obviously rolling in dough.

"Please, don't do this."

Lana's agonized whisper made his shoulders stiffen. He refused to turn around. Didn't want to see the fear and horror and disappointment on her pretty face.

"Shut up," Charlie muttered.

She ignored the order. "Please," she said again. "I'll give you anything you want, just let me go. I have money. Lots and lots of it. My father is—"

"We know exactly who your father is," Tango cut in, sounding amused. "So shut your trap and walk."

Lana made a startled noise, as if Tango had shoved her, and Deacon fought back a wave of rage. If Tango touched her one more time, Deacon would...do nothing.

Get a hold of yourself, for Chrissake.

He curled his hands into fists and looked straight ahead. This strange bout of protectiveness he felt toward Lana was unacceptable. If Le Clair got even the slightest whiff of it, Deacon would be sent packing. And he could kiss all that cash goodbye.

The foursome stepped outside. It was six in the morning, but the front of the station was bustling with people. A man walked by, talking loudly into his cell phone in a string of Italian phrases that Deacon understood perfectly. He'd been fluent in Italian for years. French, too, and Russian, Greek, Spanish, Latin… His parents had made certain he had the best education a boy could have.

That is, before his father had shot his mother in the head and proceeded to turn the gun on himself.

Deacon experienced a burst of shock as the memory crept into his consciousness. Shit. What was he doing, thinking about all that old garbage? It was over, done with. His parents were dead, but he was very much alive. And at the moment, he had a job to do.

"Echo should be waiting right over... There he is," Deacon said brusquely as a black SUV with heavily tinted windows pulled up behind one of the taxis out front.

He turned, getting another dose of the sheer betrayal sizzling in Lana's eyes. "Why are you doing this?" she pleaded softly. "How could you, after—"

A sharp shake of his head shut her up, and he had to give her credit. The gorgeous blonde stopped abruptly without finishing the sentence that would have undoubtedly revealed their carnal connection.

"Get in the car," he cut in coldly, opening the door for her.

Lana stared into the dark interior of the SUV, her reluctance creasing her delicate forehead. Deacon couldn't help but notice how beautiful and put-together she looked, despite her obvious turmoil. Her red T-shirt was wrinkle-free, her pale blond hair smoothed back in a neat ponytail. Only the trepidation in her ocean-blue eyes betrayed her composed appearance.

"Please," she whispered again.

She yelped as Charlie jammed his gun into her tailbone, practically pushing her into the vehicle. "Inside, now," Charlie snapped.

As Tango slid into the front seat next to Echo, Deacon and Charlie sandwiched Lana in the back. As soon as the doors closed, Charlie removed a long scrap of black cotton and proceeded to blindfold Lana, who protested wildly.

"No," she burst out. "Please, just let me go! I promise I won't tell anyone about this! I'll—"

"Shut up," Tango grumbled from the front seat.

Pure agony boiled in Deacon's stomach as Echo drove away from the Milan station. Lana was trembling uncontrollably beside him. Her firm thigh was pressed against his, and each tremor that rocked her body shook his, as well. His fingers tingled with the need to touch her face, offer a reassuring caress. But he'd be a dead man if he did it. The others would immediately report the transgression to Le Clair.

"Is the plane ready?" Tango was asking Echo.

Echo, a bulky man with shoulder-length black hair tied back in a low ponytail, nodded briskly. "The others are already at the airstrip. All the arrangements have been made."

Next to him, Lana let out a tiny sob. He glanced over, wincing when he noticed the tears streaming down from beneath her blindfold.

"Why are you doing this?" she asked, and he knew the question was directed at him.

He also knew she must have a dozen more questions, also for him. Fortunately, she didn't voice any of them. When Charlie ordered her to shut up again, she finally obeyed, growing silent. The trembling continued, though. And he noticed her small hands were clasped together over her abdomen, in an almost protective gesture.

The sun was just beginning to rise when the SUV arrived at the private airstrip on the out-skirts of the city. A shiny white Learjet sat majestically on the narrow, paved runway, making Deacon raise a dark brow. Le Clair's bosses really were loaded, weren't they? Most of Deacon's gigs involved rusty old Cessnas that barely got him from point A to B, not expensive private jets that probably cost millions.

Le Clair was already marching over to the vehicle before it even came to a complete stop, his thick black eyebrows creased together in distaste. The man's angular features displayed an expression of perpetual annoyance. Le Clair always seemed to be irritated by something, and patience wasn't really his strong suit. He also had a vicious temper, often triggered by the most innocuous things. But Deacon wasn't foolish enough to challenge Le Clair or point out his weaknesses. Not unless he wanted a bullet between his eyes, which Paul Le Clair was quite capable of delivering.

This was the first time Deacon had worked with the other man, but he'd been well aware of Le Clair's reputation. Vicious, greedy, dangerous as hell. A former member of the French Foreign Legion, Le Clair had been discharged thanks to his reckless violence and a cruel streak that ran far too deep. He was known to shoot his own men if they did something to displease him.

Definitely not the kind of man Deacon normally wanted to work for, but the payment for the job held great enough appeal that he'd finally accepted. But he'd been trying to stay under the man's radar since this gig started. When he'd told Le Clair that the target had made contact with him in the Louvre, he'd feared the man's reaction, prepared for anything, including violence, but Le Clair had simply shrugged and sent Charlie to take over the recon.

Which made Deacon think that this assignment was exceptionally important to the boss. None of the men had been provided with any details, but they all knew who Lana Kelley was. Her daddy was a U.S. senator, her mother was an heiress. The Kelleys even hobnobbed with the president, for Chrissake. Lots of money to be had in kidnapping a Kelley.

But Lana was a high-profile target, which meant they needed to handle this situation with the utmost delicacy. No doubt Le Clair wanted a smooth exchange, and internal grievances with his team wouldn't help his cause. So Deacon had been spared, but he'd been walking on egg-shells around the boss ever since.

"You're late," Le Clair barked as they got out of the car.

Charlie was visibly apologetic, a deep blush rising on his dark skin. "The train came in ten minutes later than scheduled."

Le Clair ignored the excuse. His shrewd silver eyes narrowed as Deacon yanked Lana out of the SUV. "She's shorter than I imagined," the boss remarked. He swept his gaze up and down Lana's slender body, frowning when he got to the open-toed sandals covering her delicate feet. "Did you bring her suitcase?"

Deacon nodded, then pulled Lana's black suitcase from the car and dropped it on the ground.

"Good." Le Clair's frown deepened. "She needs better shoes. Warmer clothing. If she didn't pack any, we'll need to stop somewhere and buy some gear for her."

Deacon's interest piqued. This was the first time Le Clair had dropped any hints about their destination. Warm clothing, better shoes. Obviously somewhere cooler. The mountains perhaps? Northern Canada?

He shoved aside the thoughts and followed the group toward the jet. Le Clair had a hand on Lana's arm, pulling her along beside him, and Deacon saw her lush pink lips tighten.

"Who are you people?" Lana demanded, her blindfolded head moving from side to side.

Le Clair chuckled. "You don't need to worry yourself with that, Miss Kelley. But if you'd like, think of us as your new caretakers."

"Not likely," she muttered.

Le Clair yanked on her arm. Hard enough that she yelped with pain.

Deacon kept his arms glued to his sides so he couldn't act on the sudden impulse to charge his boss and beat him to a bloody pulp for manhandling Lana.

"So we've got a sassy one on our hands," Le Clair muttered, sounding both amused and infuriated. "Maybe we should lay down some ground rules, Miss Kelley. Just so you know where you stand. And what might get you killed."

She released a shaky breath.

"You do exactly as we say," Le Clair continued pleasantly. "You eat when we tell you, sleep when we tell you. You don't talk back, you don't argue. You follow orders like the good girl you are, and in return, we don't shoot you. Sound reasonable?"

Lana didn't answer.

Le Clair curled his fingers over her arm and squeezed hard. "I asked you a question."

"It sounds reasonable," she wheezed out, trying to shrug out of his grasp.

Every muscle in Deacon's body coiled tight. Lana looked so small, so helpless, being dragged by Le Clair's six-foot frame. Her shoulders were hunched over, shaking ferociously, and it took all of his willpower not to pull her into his arms. Which only brought back the image of the last time he'd held her in his arms. The way he'd run his hands over the gentle curves of her body. The weight of her small, firm breasts in his palms. The relentless way she'd moved her hips beneath him.…

He smothered a groan. This was bad. Really, really bad. He couldn't seem to look at the woman without remembering her in his bed. She was supposed to be a target. A job.

The money. He had to focus on the money. He made a good deal of cash working as a merc, but this job could be his retirement. He'd spent the past twenty years fighting to survive, barely scraping by in the beginning, but he'd made a name for himself as a soldier, a man capable of handling any mission that came his way, no matter how challenging. Eventually, once he started making cash hand over fist, the challenge was what kept him going. Taking on an impossible job and executing it brought him satisfaction. Pleasure, even.

But he couldn't go on this way forever. He was thirty-eight years old. Eventually he'd have to quit risking his neck, and the money this assignment would bring in was enough to live on for the rest of his life, if he chose to get out. What would he do anyway, if he gave this all up? He'd lived fast and dangerous for so many years now, taken on jobs that most men wouldn't dream of taking, usually legal, though sometimes the lines were blurred. He'd walked the dark side for so long, he wasn't sure light belonged in his life. Maybe the darkness was all he'd ever have.

As they reached the jet, Kilo descended the metal ladder and stepped onto the tarmac. Of all the men on the team, Kilo was by the far the biggest. At six-five and two hundred and fifty pounds, the man was enormous. He also doubled as a pilot, though how he managed to wedge that huge body into the cockpit was anyone's guess.

"We're all fueled up and ready to go," Kilo announced in his Tennessee drawl. The gentle accent seemed completely wrong coming out of the guy's mouth.

"Watch your step," Le Clair said to Lana, then gave her bottom a firm slap and pushed her onto the first step.

With the blindfold on, she was unprepared for climbing stairs, and ended up stumbling forward, her hands shooting out in search of something to steady her.

Le Clair chuckled again, the harsh sound bringing a jolt of rage to Deacon's gut.

"Easy," he found himself hissing out.

Le Clair's head swiveled in his direction. Those silvery eyes narrowed. "Excuse me?"

Deacon quickly backpedaled. "Her daddy

won't be so generous if he finds out we're roughing up his daughter."

The boss raised one thick brow. "How about you leave the cash negotiating to me and get on the damn plane, Delta."

Deacon made a show of apology, bowing his head slightly and climbing up the ladder with hunched shoulders. Why hadn't he just kept his mouth shut? So what if Le Clair was being a little too rough with Lana? It was just part of the job. Shake up the target, get her nice and scared.

Except, scaring Lana was the last thing he wanted to do.

The interior of the jet was pristine, featuring two plush white leather sofas and mahogany tables. There was even a small bar in the corner. Discomfort crept up Deacon's spine. Last time he'd been on a plane like this was more than two decades ago. His father had owned a sweet little Gulfstream, which the family made good use of, traveling to their vacation homes in the Hamptons, Europe and the villa in Tahiti. Back then, Deacon had enjoyed being surrounded by such wealth. Now it only reminded him of the way his entire life had shattered.

"Put her over there," Le Clair said to Charlie, nodding toward the end of one couch. "Cuff her to the table."

Deacon tried not to cringe as Charlie hauled Lana to the sofa, forcibly made her sit, then circled one metal handcuff around a slender wrist and secured the other to the leg of the table beside her. The position had her leaning to the side, but none of the men seemed concerned with her discomfort.

Deacon pretended it didn't bother him, either. Remaining expressionless, he headed for the other couch as Echo closed the door of the jet. He was about to sit down when Le Clair issued a sharp order. "Delta, get in the cockpit with Kilo. You get to play copilot this morning."

He got the message loud and clear. Le Clair didn't want him around after the way he'd reprimanded him out on the steps. He was being banished, punished for talking out of turn.

"Yes, sir," he murmured before turning around and heading for the cockpit door.

Just as well. Maybe he could use this time to figure out what the hell to do. He needed a moment alone with Lana, so he could make sure she understood just how hazardous it would be if she revealed their liaison to the others. Maybe he could use their tryst to convince her not to cause any trouble. Get her to trust him.

Because he knew, without a doubt, how volatile Paul Le Clair's temper was. Le Clair might have use for Lana now, but if her daddy didn't pay up, she could very well end up being collateral damage.

And Deacon had no intention of letting that happen.

Chapter 3

Deacon was obviously an undercover operative. Lana reached that conclusion somewhere between being blindfolded in the SUV and being hauled off the plane. She wasn't sure how long they'd been in the air. Her captors had kept the blindfold on the entire time, which made it impossible to look at her watch, but her internal clock told her many hours had passed. At least ten. She hadn't heard Deacon's voice in the cabin during the flight, causing her to deduce that he was the "Delta" who the man with the faint French accent had ordered into the cockpit.

She sensed his presence the entire time,

though, and spent the flight piecing together the details that provided the evidence to confirm her theory. The imperceptible shake of his head when she'd been about to remind him of their night together. The reluctance in his eyes before the blindfold had been tied around her head. The way he'd told his boss to go easy on her when the man got too rough.

He was evidently working undercover. Somehow he'd infiltrated this group of thugs, and he was here to bust them. Bust them, and protect her in the meantime. That had to be it.

Right?

Guess again, Nancy Drew.

Lana ignored the cynical voice. No, that *had* to be it. Why else would Deacon be here?

To kidnap you, idiot.

No. She clamped her teeth over her bottom lip. No, he must have more honorable intentions. She might not have much experience with men, but she'd always relied on her immaculate judgment. She had a sixth sense about people.

Knew right from that very first "hello" whether they were good at heart, or working an agenda. Her brother Jim still teased her about it, calling her a walking lie-detector test. Her BS meter was flawless.

Or at least it had been in the past.

"Walk toward the car," came the voice she now recognized as Scar Cheek, or Tango as she'd heard one of the men call him.

Walk toward the car. Right, because she could totally *see* the car. The blindfold was beginning to annoy her. She was tired of being in the dark, literally.

A hand wrenched her arm, nearly ripping it from the socket. She cried out in pain, but no one consoled her. Instead, she was being dragged along again. A chill hung in the air, making goose bumps rise on her bare arms. She remembered the boss man mentioning warm clothing. Were they somewhere north? Up in the mountains? A hysterical laugh bubbled in the back of her throat. For all she knew, they'd flown her to Antarctica.

"Goddamn northern California," she heard a male voice mumble so quietly they probably didn't realize she'd heard it.

But she had. Loud and clear.

Northern California!

Okay, so she had a location. An ironic one, seeing as she'd spent the past couple of weeks fighting the urge to come back to the States. Now she was here, and her family probably had no clue. Unless her captors had contacted them already. Just as she'd deduced Deacon was one of the good guys, she also knew exactly why she was here.

Money.

Story of her life, wasn't it? She was Lana Kelley, the youngest child of two incredibly rich parents, not to mention a wealthy uncle. These men obviously wanted to squeeze some cash out of her parents, or maybe Uncle Donald. There was no other reason why she'd be kidnapped, and this was just another example of how money drove people to such incredible lengths. *Evil* lengths.

Lana drew in a wobbly breath as someone shoved her into the backseat of another vehicle. She wanted to speak, to assure these men that whatever they wanted, her family would give them, but she was afraid. Frenchie, the boss man who'd met them at the airfield, had made it clear what would happen if she gave him any trouble. So she held her tongue. They would make their demands known soon, and she knew once her family learned of her disappearance, they would move heaven and earth to find her.

"Did you get the clothes I asked for?" came Frenchie's muffled voice.

A baritone voice recited an answer. "Sweaters, jeans, parka, wool socks. Got it all, boss."

"Good."

The sound of an engine roaring to life filled Lana's ears, and then the vehicle began to move. This car ride was bumpier than the one

in Milan. Either the road was riddled with pot-
holes, or they were venturing into rough terrain.
Definitely the mountains, if they truly were in
northern California.

Lana spent the ride cataloging the voices and
faces she'd come across, trying to figure out
how many people were involved in this kidnapping. Deacon, she knew. Tango and Cold
Eyes had been on the train. Frenchie and someone named Echo at the airstrip. The pilot, Kilo
or Keemo—she hadn't been able to make out
the name. And now Baritone. That added up to
seven men.

Eight, she amended, when the car came to a
sharp halt what seemed like hours later. One
last voice had joined the mix as she was thrust
from the car by her armpits. Eight men had con-
spired to take her by force and whisk her to another country. Well, only seven, perhaps, if her
suspicions about Deacon proved correct.

A hand suddenly touched the side of her head.

"Bite me and I'll tear your throat out," came the voice she now recognized as Echo's.

He was undoing her blindfold, to her instant relief.

"She won't bite," she heard Cold Eyes remark, a smirk in his voice. "This one's a pussycat."

Pussycat, her butt! Just wait until she got the chance to escape. She might look small and fragile, but Lana had been trained in self-defense since the age of twelve. Her older brothers had made sure of it, in case she ever found herself in a position where she needed to protect herself.

Sort of like this one.

The blindfold came loose and Lana blinked a few times, letting her eyes adjust to the sudden burst of light. Italy was nine hours ahead of California, and they'd left Milan at 6:00 a.m.... Lana quickly did the math. It must be nine in the morning now, here in California.

She examined her surroundings, as well as the faces of the men responsible for taking her against her will. She'd been right—they were in the mountains. The car had brought them to a rocky clearing, barren save for the yellowing grass. Dylan had mentioned that a drought had been plaguing the northern part of the state, and the dying grass showed the strain of that. Several yards away stood a single-story cabin, the size of a modest bungalow. Made of dark weathered logs, the cabin boasted a paint-chipped green door and two boarded-up windows. In the distance the mountains loomed, majestic peaks standing proud against a cloudless, clear-blue backdrop. The scenery would almost be beautiful, if she weren't in such an ugly situation.

She glanced at her kidnappers, already familiar with Deacon, Tango and Cold Eyes. The other five were interchangeable—big, bulky men in heavy sweaters and warm pants, weapons strapped all over their muscular bodies. She focused on Frenchie, who was easy to pick out of the crowd by the constant orders he barked out at everyone. Some of the men began carrying gear into the cabin, while others were ordered to "secure the perimeter." Lana stared at Frenchie, memorizing every last feature.

He wasn't unattractive, but not handsome, either. His features were too sharp, too feral, and though he wasn't as bulky as some of the others, his tall, wiry frame radiated strength. And danger. Oh, yeah, this man was extremely dangerous.

Frenchie caught her staring, and scowled in her direction. Then he turned his head and looked around at the other men, as if gauging his options. Lana's heart leaped when Frenchie nodded at Deacon and said, "Get her inside. Back room."

"Yes, sir," Deacon mumbled.

She was being manhandled again, but this time she didn't protest. Finally she would be alone with Deacon. Finally she could get some damn answers.

Deacon's large hand was warm on her bare

arm. He towered over her as they walked toward the narrow front door of the cabin. Her traitorous eyes couldn't help staring at his incredible body, the snug fit of his trousers. Even now, while caught up in the most terrifying situation, she was aware of his innate sexiness, his primal virility.

What was *wrong* with her?

The moment they were out of earshot, Lana opened her mouth, but Deacon glanced over and muttered, "Quiet. Not yet."

Her mouth snapped shut. Apparently Deacon was just as good at delivering orders as his boss, but again she didn't object. A few more seconds weren't going to kill her.

These men, on the other hand…

They entered the cabin, and a musty stench immediately filled Lana's nostrils. She made a face. They couldn't invest in some air freshener? The main room was dark and it took a few moments for her eyes to adjust. When they did, she realized the cabin didn't look any better than it smelled. It consisted of one large room, which had a crumbling stone fireplace, three torn couches and a table that sagged. There was a small kitchen on one side, a dark corridor on the other.

Holding her suitcase as if it weighed only a couple of measly pounds, Deacon led her down the hallway, which featured three doorways. As ordered, he took her to the room at the very end of the hall, pushed open the door and gestured for her to enter.

Lana reluctantly walked inside, slightly pleased to find that this room smelled better than the one out front. Like pine cleaner and Windex, as if it had been cleaned recently.

The thought brought a tremor of panic. Had the room been cleaned in anticipation of a guest? As in *her?* She glanced around her, studying the single bed against one wood-paneled wall, the little desk under the window and the thick white shag carpet beneath her sandaled feet.

And then she spun around to face Deacon, who quietly closed the door behind them.

Their eyes locked. Silence fell over the room, hanging there for several seconds, until Lana finally exploded.

"Why the *hell* are you doing this to me, Deacon Holt?"

Deacon cringed as his name, his real full name, snapped out of Lana's mouth like a sharp round from a shotgun. She sounded absolutely livid, and he couldn't help but notice how cute she looked with her cheeks flushed in anger. He pushed aside the inappropriate thought and focused on her blue eyes. He had no idea where to start, or how he could possibly explain himself and his actions to this woman.

So he just stood there, his mouth half open, his brain working overtime trying to find a way to make this right.

Uh-huh. Because making this *right* was actually a legitimate option.

Fortunately, Lana spoke again before he could say anything, though when he heard the words, he realized there was nothing fortunate about it.

"You're a cop, right?" she said urgently.

His eyebrows shot north. A cop? She actually thought he was a cop?

"Undercover," she went on. "You're pretending to be in cahoots with these jerks so you can arrest them, right?"

A headache formed at his temples. Christ. The hope flashing across her face was almost painful. He dreaded having to burst that optimistic bubble.

"You're going to get me out of here. *Right?*"

The pleading note to her voice did him in. He broke the eye contact, turning his head to focus on the splintered old desk beneath the window. He knew Le Clair had been trying to punish him by assigning him babysitting duty, and he felt wholly punished. Not because he'd gotten stuck with a task that most soldiers despised, since coddling targets was always a pain in the ass, but because he now had to explain to the woman he'd taken to bed that she was wrong. That he was, in fact, one of those "jerks" she spoke of with such vehemence.

"Deacon," she begged softly.

He found the courage to look at her again. "No."

A beat of silence. "No, what? No, you *are* in cahoots with them, or no, you won't get me out?"

A pained sigh left his throat. "No to both."

Horror flooded her eyes. "You're not a cop?" she whispered.

He shook his head.

"You're…you're *part* of this?"

He nodded.

The horror turned to rage. Her petite body began to shake in violent shudders.

"Lana—" he started.

"Don't you dare say my name!" she roared. "If you want to call me something, call me Miss Kelley, just like my other kidnappers."

"Keep your voice down," he said sharply.

"Why?" she taunted. A humorless laugh popped out of her mouth. "So the others don't find out you had sex with your hostage? So you don't get fired?"

That pesky spark of guilt ignited in his gut again. He forced himself to ignore it. Fine, so he'd slept with the woman he'd been assigned to tail. Nobody ever said he was an honorable man. In fact, honor played no part in his life. Had it been honorable for his father to murder his mother? Had it been honorable for his uncle to steal Deacon's inheritance? Hell, no. His entire genetic code had dishonor programmed into it.

"So we don't get killed," he corrected, in harsh reply to her demand. "If Le Clair finds out about that night, he'll either fire me or kill me, and then you'll be all alone here. If he decides to kill you, too, I won't be here to stop him."

Another laugh. "You just said you're not here to save me. How do I know you wouldn't just let him kill me anyway, even if you were standing right beside him?"

"I promise you, I won't let that happen."

She went quiet for a moment, and when she spoke again, disgust laced her voice. "Jeez, I actually believe you. What is *wrong* with me? I slept with a criminal, for God's sake. You're *kidnapping* me! Why should I believe anything you say?"

"Because it's the truth," he said simply. "As long as I'm here, I won't let anyone hurt you."

Those big blue eyes searched his face. "You mean it."

He swallowed. "Yes."

"You don't want me hurt."

"No," he agreed.

"Then let me go," she pleaded. "Please, Deacon, let me go."

"I…can't." Weariness spilled into his body. "I know you don't understand any of this, but you need to cooperate with these men. You can't antagonize them. They wouldn't hesitate to shoot you, Lana. I promise you that."

Her bottom lip began to tremble.

Deacon forced himself to stay still, not to eliminate the short distance between them and take her in his arms.

"How long are you going to keep me here?" she whispered.

"I don't know," he said honestly. "Your family will be contacted soon, and I assume the exchange will happen shortly after that."

"The exchange? You mean, extorting money from my father?" Her tone rang with bitterness.

He nodded ruefully.

"I…never took you for greedy," she finally said, her dark blond eyelashes coated with sparkling moisture. "That night at the museum, you acted like money didn't matter to you."

"No, I picked up on the fact that money doesn't matter to *you*."

"So this is why you're doing this, for the money?" She shook her head, a slow sad gesture that made him uncomfortable. "I must have misjudged you."

His discomfort grew. She sounded so disappointed, a tad judgmental, too, and it was the judgment that raised his hackles. What did this woman know about poverty? Had she ever lived on the streets? Sat on a sidewalk holding out a tin can, begging for coins? She lived in splendor now, but had that splendor ever been taken away? He knew all about the life Lana Kelley led. The Beverly Hills mansion, the Montana ranch, the numerous vacation homes. He'd lived it, too. He'd been the son of a shipping tycoon, for Chrissake.

And he'd lost everything. Every last thing, save for the clothes on his back and the small duffel his uncle had let him pack before kicking him out on the street.

Lana Kelley didn't know what life without money was. She'd never had to fight for her own survival.

And she had no right to judge him.

"Put on some warmer clothing." He moved stiffly to the door. "You must be hungry after that long flight. I'll bring you some food."

"Wait."

His hand froze on the door handle. Slowly, he turned around. Her face was pale, her eyes weary with defeat.

"I don't care what your motives are," she said in a miserable voice. "But if you want money, I'll give you money. I promise, whatever—what did you call him? Le Clair?—well, whatever he's paying you, I'll double it. Just help me get out of here and I'll make sure you have all the money you want."

He stifled a sigh. Double the pay? The offer might have been tempting, if not for the fact that Le Clair would hunt him down and murder him if he ever defected.

He said as much to Lana, eyeing her unhappily. "Le Clair is a very dangerous man. A man you don't cross. As much as I want to help you, I—"

"You don't want to help me," she cut in angrily. "If you did, you wouldn't have kidnapped me. You wouldn't have—" She stopped abruptly, a suspicious expression filling her face. "Did you know who I was, that night in the Louvre? Were you planning this, even then?"

Deacon wanted to lie. It bothered him that his first instinct was to protect this woman, even from the ugly truth. But although he was many things, a liar he wasn't.

"I knew," he replied gruffly.

She blinked, and the tears sticking to her lashes broke free and slid down her smooth cheeks. "You knew," she echoed.

"Yes." He found himself giving a hurried explanation. "But I didn't plan for us to…be intimate. I was only supposed to watch you." His voice cracked, and he cleared his throat, annoyed with the sign of weakness. "But then you spoke to me, and…well, it just happened."

Her tears fell harder. "I can't believe this. I can't…" She looked at him with tearstained cheeks, suddenly appearing much younger than her twenty-four years. "Don't let them hurt me," she finally whispered, her arms encircling her own waist and tightening over her stomach. "Just promise me that."

He tore his gaze from her and turned the doorknob. "I'll make sure nothing happens to you, Lana. I promise." Then he slid out the door and, ignoring the ache in his chest, locked it behind him.

Chapter 4

Lana's first night as an official hostage went by without incident. After Deacon left her in the back bedroom, she'd changed into jeans and a fleece hooded sweatshirt, as well as the thick wool socks her kidnappers had purchased for her. Then she'd sat on the narrow bed and catalogued every item in her suitcase. Clothes, toiletries, sewing kit, nail kit. The two kits had been confiscated by Cold Eyes, whose name was apparently Charlie. With two brothers in the military, she was familiar with the military alphabet, which Le Clair had evidently decided to employ for code names. For some reason, though, Le Clair wasn't hiding his real name from her. Almost as if he believed he were invincible, that even if she knew his true identity, it wouldn't make a damn bit of difference.

That worried her, though not as much as the fact that none of the kidnappers bothered to disguise their faces from her. Did that mean they planned to kill her? Or, like Le Clair, were these men confident that knowing what they looked like wouldn't make a difference once their assignment ended?

The last item on her growing Why-I-Should-Worry list was the pregnancy. She hadn't revealed her condition to her captors, didn't even know if she should, and though she now had the opportunity to tell Deacon, she wasn't sure she wanted the man to have any part in this baby's life. He'd kidnapped her, for God's sake. What kind of father figure was that for her child?

She was also concerned about how she would take care of herself. She hadn't been to a doctor yet, but she knew vitamins and a healthy diet were important to the growth of a healthy fetus. Hopefully she wouldn't be here for much longer, but in the meantime, she could keep taking her multivitamins, which had calcium and vitamin C and a bunch of other important nutrients. No folic acid, but again, she probably wasn't going to be here long.

As promised, Deacon had brought in some food, a surprisingly healthy dish of rice, chicken breast and broccoli. Afterward, he'd left her alone, and now she was lying down and wishing she were anywhere but here. A single bulb dangling from the ceiling illuminated the small room, and it was dark outside the window over the desk. Getting colder, too. Lana shivered on the bed, though she had a feeling the chill running through her had nothing to do with the temperature and everything to do with her predicament.

Bitterness lodged in her throat as she remembered Deacon's confession. He'd *known* who she was the night at the Louvre. He'd already been part of this sick plot to kidnap her, and yet he'd still gone ahead and made love to her.

"No," she said aloud, a vicious taste entering her mouth.

It wasn't making love. It was sex. And deception.

How was she ever going to explain this to her child when he or she got older?

The sound of the lock creaking open caught her attention. She sat up just as Deacon walked into the room. He wore dark pants and a black turtleneck underneath an unbuttoned navy-blue shirt, and for a moment she almost forgot why they were both here. He was so damn gorgeous. It wasn't fair for him to look so good and yet be doing this to her.

"I thought you might be cold," he said gruffly.

He held out his hands, and she noticed the flannel afghan. She forced herself not to feel pleasure from the thoughtful gesture.

"Thank you," she said in a stiff voice.

Deacon walked to the bed and handed her the

blanket, which she draped over her lower body. Immediately, she felt warmer.

"Lana…" he started, then stopped.

She met his hazel eyes. "Did you contact my father?"

"Not yet."

"How long am I going to be here?" There was a petulant chord to her tone, but she wasn't ashamed of it. She deserved to be childish, if she chose to be. These people had *kidnapped* her, after all.

"I don't know." He shifted uneasily. "Did you give any thought to what I told you?"

She tightened her lips. "About keeping my mouth shut?"

"Yes." That grave glimmer filled his eyes. "Everything I said was true. If Le Clair finds out about us, it won't bode well for either one of us."

She didn't doubt that. Le Clair struck her as the kind of man who'd kill Deacon in cold blood if he found out about his indiscretion. Pathetic as it was, she didn't want anything happening to Deacon. He might be in league with these men, but she'd believed him when he'd said he would keep her safe. His presence brought her a sick sense of security. If he was gone, she'd be all alone and at the mercy of Le Clair.

"I won't say anything," she finally said. A pause. "For now."

He offered an expression of gratitude. "Thank you. I know I don't deserve it."

"No, you don't."

His big shoulders sagged. "I'm sorry you're going through this. I really am. But it will all be over soon, Lana."

Anger climbed up her chest, making her throat go tight. "Don't bother with apologies. If you really cared about me, you would let me go." She frowned. "Actually, if you cared, you wouldn't have even let it get to this point. You could've warned me at the museum, told me to get out of town."

His features were creased with exhaustion as

he said, "It wouldn't have mattered. We would have found you eventually."

We. His use of the word only served as a reminder of who he truly was. He was working with these men. Holding her captive. All so he could score a few bucks. It was perplexing, because even now, she couldn't bring herself to call this man greedy. He lacked that hungry glint in his eyes, the one that every other man in this nasty group seemed to possess.

"Why do you need the money?" she blurted out, unable to let go of the disturbing notion.

Deacon shrugged. "Why don't I?"

"Are you planning on buying a yacht? A fancy villa? Cars, women, expensive gadgets?"

Discomfort was written all over his face. "No, I'm not planning on buying any of those things."

"Then *why?*"

His mouth opened, then closed, his strong throat bobbing as he swallowed repeatedly. Her question seemed to bring him great distress, which only piqued her curiosity. No, it wasn't curiosity, she quickly amended. She didn't want to know a damn thing about this man. But if she could figure out what made him tick, she might be able to use it to her advantage.

Unfortunately, he decided to ignore the question altogether. "If you need anything during the night, to use the bathroom, a glass of water... just knock on the door," he said in a rough voice.

"Deacon," she called after him, but he was already gone.

As the door closed and the lock slid back into place, Lana sagged against the uncomfortable wooden headboard of the bed.

And started to cry.

She was trying to be quiet, but Deacon clearly heard Lana's muffled sobs as he walked down the narrow hallway toward the living area. He'd made her cry. Somehow, that notion brought a slice of pain to his chest. A part of him wanted to turn around and comfort her, but he fought the urge. Damn it. He was losing control here.

Lana's question continued to buzz around in his brain like a relentless hornet. *Then why? Why did he need the money? Why was he doing this?*

He almost wished he'd gone along with her accusations, lied and told her it was all about greed. But it wasn't. Everything he was doing now, everything he'd done in the past, could all be credited to one simple thing: survival. He did what he did in order to survive. In order to ensure that never again would he be defenseless. Powerless.

Is that really why?

Deacon faltered. Truth was, a part of him wasn't even sure why he still did this. He didn't have buckets of money, but he had enough to live on modestly if he wanted to. He wasn't a scared and hungry teenager anymore, desperate to survive. He didn't need to take on so many assignments, especially not ones like this, that made him so damn uneasy.

So why?

Because you're a bad person.

The little voice spoke in a flat, unyielding tone. It was a conclusion he'd reached years ago, after spending too many nights lying in bed and wondering how on earth he'd gotten to this point. He supposed he could always quit. But then what? He'd spent too many years living dangerously, often on the wrong side of the law—no way could he quit now and live as a respectable citizen.

This attraction for Lana was going to get him in trouble, he knew that. Yet he couldn't stop it. Couldn't control the ripples of desire that shook his body each time he was in the same room as her, or the way his palms tingled, begging him to touch her. Or how every cell in his body screamed for him to whisk her away from all this. To keep her safe and protected and... happy. He wanted to make her happy.

God help him.

"How's the girl?" Le Clair demanded when Deacon stepped into the living room.

Echo and Kilo were sprawled on the two couches, catching some shut-eye before they relieved the others, who were patrolling the perimeter. Le Clair ran a tight ship, and his men were nothing if not efficient. Trip wire had been laid around the cabin, which would go kaboom if anyone tried to get near it. Motion sensors were installed on every window, and the entire interior was rigged with explosives, too, designed to eliminate evidence in case they needed to get out in a hurry. They hadn't bothered with cameras, since the area was so deserted they'd easily see or hear anyone approaching.

Tango and Charlie were stationed up in the hills, sniper rifles at hand and eyes on the clearing below, while Yankee and Oscar walked the perimeter, armed to the teeth. The sleeping beauties, Echo and Kilo, would man the next shift, and Le Clair had taken up residence on the front porch, muttering into his cell phone for most of the evening.

Deacon, of course, was on babysitting duty, though he was secretly grateful for the task. For some reason, he didn't want any of the other men around Lana.

"She's getting ready to go to sleep," Deacon informed the boss. "I'll stand guard outside the door for the night."

Le Clair looked pleased. "Good."

"I'll just use the john and then—"

"First we need to talk," the boss cut in.

Le Clair gestured for Deacon to follow him out on the rickety old porch. They stepped outside, and the wood beneath Deacon's feet creaked in protest from the weight of his black boots.

"You came highly recommended, Holt," Le Clair began, sounding wary. "But that stunt you pulled at the airstrip… I won't tolerate that insubordination, understand?"

Deacon gave a humble nod. "I know. I was completely out of line, and I promise you, boss, it won't happen again."

Those silver eyes fixed Deacon with a deadly look. "You have the hots for her, don't you?"

Deacon's head snapped up in surprise. "What? Of course not."

Le Clair chuckled. "Don't apologize for it. Even I've noticed she's a sweet piece of ass. And if this were any other job, I might even be lenient about it, let you have some fun with the girl."

Deacon swallowed down the bile suddenly coating his throat. Fun? Was he actually hearing this? Though he couldn't say it surprised him that Le Clair had given his men free rein with the targets in the past. He was simply that sadistic.

"But this one's different." Le Clair's face went grave. "She's high-profile, and we can't bring her back to her daddy carrying some bastard child because you knocked her up while taking your jollies. You hear me?"

"I hear you," Deacon muttered.

"So keep your hands off her, and don't give me any more trouble, all right?"

"Yes, sir."

"Good. Now get back inside and man the door." Le Clair suddenly let out a laugh and glanced at Deacon with surprising sympathy. "Not your ideal assignment, is it, Holt?"

"What do you mean?" Deacon asked, wary.

"I know you'd rather be out with the other men, walking the perimeter, instead of hand-holding a rich princess. I admit, I gave you the job to punish you for your earlier outburst, but it seems like our sweet Miss Kelley responds well to you."

If you only knew...

"She hasn't caused any trouble thus far, so I'm inclined to keep her under your watch." Le Clair's eyes narrowed. "You don't have a problem with that, do you?"

"Not at all, sir," Deacon said quickly.

"Good." Le Clair pulled his cell phone from

the back pocket of his black pants, and with that, the conversation was over.

With a nod, Deacon headed back inside, where he leaned against the door for a moment, collecting his composure. He knew Le Clair didn't suspect a thing, but the man's taunt about Deacon having the "hots" for Lana Kelley had hit the mark. *Hot* was precisely how he felt toward the woman. Just the sight of her made his groin tighten.

And the knowledge that Le Clair had also noticed Lana's ethereal beauty sent uneasiness soaring through him. If Le Clair even *looked* at her the wrong way, Deacon wasn't sure what he would do. He'd promised to keep her safe, and he had no intention of letting Le Clair get his grubby hands on her.

But he couldn't challenge Le Clair, either. From the moment Deacon had accepted this gig, he'd known it wouldn't be like the others. The people he'd worked for in the past were innocent little lambs compared to Paul Le Clair. The man was a stone-cold killer, with a total disregard for other human beings, not to mention a complete lack of restraint. If Lana so much as sneezed wrong, Le Clair wouldn't hesitate to kill her, and that troubled the hell out of Deacon.

God, his head was spinning. It was becoming tiring, trying to stay focused on this job. He had Le Clair breathing down his neck, Lana gazing at him with those betrayed blue eyes, his conscience yelling at him for his part in this, his brain reminding him that survival and self-preservation should always come first.

It was getting hard keeping it together, and the assignment had just begun.

How on earth was he going to see it through without going absolutely freaking insane?

The loud ringing of her cell phone drew Sarah Mistler Kelley from a troubled sleep. Instantly alert, she reached for the phone, which she'd set on the antique mahogany nightstand by the luxurious bed in the guest room of Vivienne

Kemp's rambling beach house. Sarah had been staying with her old friend ever since the news of her husband's infidelities hit the tabloids. The wife of a senator, Sarah had gotten used to being hounded by the press.

But never for this reason.

Swallowing down the golf-ball-size lump in the back of her throat, Sarah glanced at the caller ID. Her bitterness heightened. Hank. The number flashing across the screen of her BlackBerry was that of her husband's cell phone—it was not the long-distance number she'd been hoping for.

Sighing, she set the phone back down. Hank had been calling non-stop since she'd walked out of their Beverly Hills mansion. She'd diligently avoided each call, and tonight would be no different.

Sarah leaned against the headboard, listening to the sound of the waves crashing against the wooden stilts beneath the enormous house. The ocean was choppy tonight, as turbulent as her emotions. A terrible feeling had been gnawing at the pit of her stomach since yesterday evening, when her daughter hadn't phoned as she'd promised.

Lana was a big girl, Sarah was well aware of that, but a part of her still wasn't able to accept it. Lana would always be her baby, the tiny miracle that had come to her when she'd considered herself too old to bear any more children. And she'd forever have a soft spot for her youngest, the lone female after a long line of big, strapping boys.

The phone rang again, making her jump. She'd opted for a utilitarian ring tone, unlike the fancy Mozart symphony her husband had chosen for his phone. Hank Kelley was all about flash. Always had been, always would be.

Sarah's lips tightened when she saw his number again. Twice in two minutes. The man must be getting desperate.

"Good," she muttered to herself.

He deserved to feel desperate, after the way he'd treated her.

The ringing stopped, but the relief she experienced didn't last long, as the phone came to life again a second later.

Concern sparked in her belly. This couldn't be good. Three calls. Biting back her anger, she picked up the phone and said, "What do you want, Hank?"

"Sarah! Thank God!"

Her body instantly tensed, and not just because she was talking to her estranged husband. There was deep worry lining that gruff voice— and Hank wasn't prone to worrying. When a problem arose, he brushed it off, letting someone else take care of it, and it was usually his wife who ended up cleaning his messes.

"What's wrong?" she asked immediately. "Is it one of the children?"

He paused for a long beat. "Have you spoken to Lana?"

That nagging feeling that had plagued her for more than a day came rushing back. "No, I haven't. She was supposed to call me yesterday when she got to Florence, but she never did."

"I was afraid of that."

Sarah clutched the phone tighter, her knuckles turning white from the force of her grip. "What's going on, Hank? Do you know why Lana didn't call me?"

There was a deafening silence.

"Hank."

"She's disappeared," he finally said.

Sarah's heart stopped. "What do you mean, she's disappeared?"

"She boarded the train in Paris, and nobody has seen her since. And this morning...I got a call."

Terror swept through her like a flash flood. "Who from?"

"I don't know." Her husband sounded so distressed she had to fight a spark of sympathy. "Whoever it was, he said he's got Lana. I didn't believe him at first, but I've been calling around and I can't find her, damn it! Her landlord said she hasn't been back at her flat, her professors haven't heard from her…it's like she vanished into thin air."

A chill shuddered through Sarah's body. "I knew something was wrong," she whispered. "When she didn't call…I *felt* something was wrong. Oh, God. Hank, who could have taken her?"

Another beat. "We both know I have a lot of enemies, darling."

Anger exploded in her stomach, not just because he'd called her darling, when, at the moment, he had no right to call her *anything* of the sort, but because she knew if Lana had disappeared, it was all Hank Kelley's fault.

"What enemies?" she demanded. "Who has her?"

"I…don't know."

He was lying to her. Sarah had given this man more than thirty years of her life. She knew him better than he knew himself. And she *always* knew when he was lying.

"What did you do?" she asked coldly.

He sounded dismayed. "Darling, I—"

"Don't you dare *darling* me! Tell me, what kind of mess have you gotten yourself into this time, and what does it have to do with our daughter?"

"It's…complicated."

"Complicated?" She was practically roaring now, but was far too upset to lower her voice. Vivienne's bedroom was on the floor above hers, and she prayed she didn't wake her long-time friend. "Our daughter has disappeared, and you know something about it! So you better *un*complicate it and tell me the damn truth. What exactly did the caller say?"

"I told you, just that he has Lana, and that if we call the police, there will be repercussions."

Sarah paled. "They'll kill her?"

"That's what I'm afraid of." He hesitated. "We can't contact the police yet, not until the man calls back."

Sarah gave an unladylike curse. "So you want to sit around and wait?"

"I'm going to get her back, Sarah."

The confidence ringing in his tone made her want to hit something. "Sure you will," she spat out. "You constantly bring all these problems on our family, promise to take care of them and, in the end, you only cause a greater rift between us. Cole can barely look at you! Chase refuses to have any contact with us, depriving me of my only grandchildren! And now Lana is gone."

Sarah fought for breath. She was suddenly seeing stars, the turmoil of the past few weeks finally beginning to take its toll on her. Her husband had cheated on her, after she'd given him years and years of devotion, and now, because of some foolhardy decision he'd made, their only daughter was missing.

"You had better get her back," she warned, her hands shaking so badly she could barely hold the phone steady anymore. "Do you hear me, Hank Kelley? You've done a lot of awful things in your lifetime. You've hurt me more than I can ever say. But I swear to you, Hank, if anything happens to our baby girl, I will never forgive you for this. *Never.*"

Chapter 5

Four days. Lana could barely comprehend how four days had passed and she was still being kept against her will in a desolate cabin in northern California. Why hadn't the kidnappers contacted her family yet? Or maybe they had, and her family was refusing to negotiate with them....

She forced the scary thought from her mind, fixing her gaze out the small rusted window in the bedroom. No, her father would never stand for this. Hank Kelley, despite his many flaws, would never allow his daughter to be held captive for a second longer than necessary. Maybe

Le Clair was the one stalling. He could always be holding out for more money.

More money for what, though? What was this even about? A straight-up ransom thing? Or did it have to do with her dad's recent scandal? Could Le Clair be blackmailing Hank—maybe threatening to reveal some more damaging information? None of this made sense to her. There were no answers, no clarity. Just the knowledge that she was a prisoner.

Moving to the window of the bedroom, Lana examined the barren land through the dirty windowpane. Her pulse quickened when she caught sight of Charlie standing several yards away, a rifle slung over his shoulder and his shaved head gleaming in the pale afternoon sun. The man's dark gaze was sharp as a hawk's, moving left and right in a practiced sweep of the area. She suspected the others had taken up similar positions to guard the cabin.

To make sure nobody approached unseen—and that she couldn't escape.

Trapped. She was utterly trapped, and a rush of pure helplessness hit her body. Her hands slid down to her still-flat belly, stroking it protectively.

"It's okay, baby," she whispered. "We're going to get out of this."

She'd begun talking to the baby often over the days. She hoped he or she was finding her voice reassuring. It reassured her, too, despite the fact that she'd never been prone to talking to herself.

"Your granddaddy is going to pay the bad men whatever they want," she continued softly, stroking her stomach. "And then we'll go home. You're going to love your grandparents' house. It's big and beautiful and you'll have so much room to play...."

Her voice drifted, as she realized she had no clue if she and the baby would even live in the Beverly Hills mansion. She probably ought to get her own place, or maybe find a cozy little ranch house in Montana, near the Bar Lazy K, her brother Cole's ranch. But her mother would probably want her close by. Mom would adore being a grandma. Her eldest brother, Chase, had two kids with his wife, but Lana's mother didn't get to see them often. Only once a year, when she flew out to Chase's cattle station in Australia. Chase hadn't returned to the States since he'd left at the age of eighteen, determined to be rid of his father.

Lana didn't understand her older brother's decision. Their dad might not be the best paternal role model, but he was still family. She had no intention of ever abandoning her family the way Chase had.

God, she missed them. Cole and Dylan, the handsome serious twins. Jake, with his reckless love of adventure. Jim, only a year older than her and yet her biggest protector. And her mother. God, she wondered how Mom was faring. First the shocking revelation of Hank's affairs and now her daughter kidnapped.

Tears stung Lana's eyes. She moved away

from the window, just as the lock clicked and the door swung open. Deacon's broad frame filled the doorway. He held a small plate loaded with thin slices of carrots and celery.

"I thought you might want a snack," he said, his features creased with hesitation.

She swiped at her tears with the sleeve of her burgundy mohair sweater. "Thanks," she said dully, sinking onto the edge of the bed.

Deacon handed her the plate, and though she was too depressed to eat, she mechanically bit into one carrot and forced herself to chew. The baby needed nourishment, and she refused to deprive it of a solitary thing. So far, she hadn't experienced any morning sickness, which was fortunate. She had no clue how she'd explain it to Deacon, who would be the one taking her to and from the bathroom if her stomach began to rebel.

"How are you doing?" he asked.

"Gee, *Delta.*" She used the name she heard the other men call him, mostly out of spite. "I'm doing great. I'm locked up in a tiny room. I'm not allowed to go outside. I get all my meals brought in to me like I'm a naughty child who can't eat with the grown-ups. I've been kidnapped. By a man I had sex with, no less. Oh, and my back hurts. Any other questions?"

"You'd like to go outside?"

She faltered. Seriously? Out of everything she'd just unloaded on him, *that* was what he hung on to? But she decided to dial down on the anger. Truth was, she was tired of being cooped up inside.

"Yes, actually, I would."

"Put on your coat then. It's windy out there."

She hid her shock. Not wanting to look a gift horse in the mouth, she set the plate down on the desk and reached for the knee-length red parka her captors had given her. She had a feeling red was a deliberate choice of color. She'd be more likely to stand out in this bland landscape if she tried to run.

She put on the coat, zipped it up to the neck,

then undid her ponytail and let her hair loose. She noticed Deacon watching her with an indefinable expression, his serious eyes resting on the long blond tresses falling over her shoulders.

"What?" she said, oddly defensive.

He cleared his throat. "Nothing. Come on, let's go."

She didn't object as he took her arm and led her out the door. She suspected idyllic strolls in the mountains weren't what Le Clair had had in mind when he'd arranged to kidnap her, and she was grateful that Deacon was being so nice about it.

Nice?

She'd obviously gone nuts. There was nothing nice about any of this. She was a prisoner, for Pete's sake.

"Stockholm syndrome," she mumbled under her breath.

Deacon cocked his head. "What?"

"Nothing."

When they entered the living room, Lana saw

Tango, aka Scar Cheek, lying on one couch, while the enormous man she now recognized as Kilo sat in a ratty old recliner, his eyes closed. Those eyes snapped open the moment Deacon and Lana entered, and a harsh scowl immediately spread across the man's mouth.

"What's she doing out here?" Kilo demanded, glaring at Deacon.

"Getting some air," Deacon replied lightly.

"Does the boss know about this?"

"He will soon." Deacon kept his tone casual as he walked Lana to the front door.

The moment they stepped on the porch, a gust of wind slammed into her, making her hair blow around in all directions. But the chill of the breeze was nothing compared to the cold gunmetal-gray eyes they encountered.

"What's going on here, Delta?" Le Clair snapped when he caught sight of them. He'd been sitting on a white wicker chair with a cell phone in his hand, but he stood the moment they came outside.

"Miss Kelley requested some air," Deacon said quietly. "I didn't think you'd object."

Le Clair's gaze zeroed in on Lana, then rested on the tight grip of Deacon's hand on her arm. After a second, his features relaxed and he gave a shrug. "Fine. Make it quick."

"Yes, sir."

They descended the creaky porch steps and ventured farther, their boots crunching against the stiff dead grass as they walked across it.

"How can you answer to that man?" Lana muttered, keeping her voice low so it didn't carry with the wind.

"I have no choice. Everyone answers to someone, Lana."

"Well, I'd never work for a man like that. He's evil." The wind snaked its way under her hair, lifting stray strands and whipping them around. "Has my father been contacted yet?"

Deacon hesitated.

"Well?" she demanded.

"Yes."

The admission seemed difficult for him, and it surprised the hell out of Lana. So her dad knew about the kidnapping? He *knew* and he'd sat around twiddling his thumbs for four days now?

A terrifying thought slid into her head. "Is he refusing to pay?"

"I don't think so."

"You don't think so?" she echoed. She stopped walking, planting her hands on her hips. "What is going on, Deacon? You said this was about money."

"It is." His tone didn't sound so convincing anymore.

Fear gathered in Lana's stomach. "Then why am I still here? Why hasn't an exchange been made?"

His chest rose as he drew in a long breath. "I don't know," he repeated.

Silence fell between them. They began to walk again, moving around the small clearing. Lana could feel Le Clair's gaze on them, and the tiny hairs on the back of her neck tingled. In the distance, the mountains towered over the landscape almost ominously, and yet they brought a strange sense of comfort. At least she had an idea of where she was. If she got the chance to speak to her family, she knew she needed to figure out a way to give them a clue of her whereabouts.

Trying to be discreet, she glanced around, looking at the bushes across the clearing, the scattering of boulders to her left. Maybe if she could find a way out of the bedroom in the middle of the night, she could run toward those rocks and—

"Don't even think about it," Deacon said sternly.

She guiltily avoided his eyes. "I don't know what you're talking about."

"You're plotting your escape." He let out a heavy sigh. "There are motion sensors rigged all over this mountain, Lana. Outside your window, too. You'd only be wasting your time."

She tried to hide the disappointment weighing down on her chest. Well, at least she'd tried.

She and Deacon came to a stop underneath a cluster of tall redwood trees with knotted branches and thick leaves. The sun had disappeared behind a patch of gray clouds, and it was cooler beneath the trees. Lana tucked her hands into the pockets of her coat, shivering slightly.

"You're cold. We should go in," Deacon said roughly.

"No," she protested. "Don't put me back in the room. Not yet." She leaned against the gnarled brown bark of one of the tree trunks and glanced at him warily. "Did you really grow up in Boston?"

He looked surprised by the question. "Yeah, I did."

"So that wasn't a lie?"

"No. I'm from the east coast, like I said." He shrugged. "Though I haven't been back there in two decades."

"Why not?" She immediately berated herself

for the display of curiosity. He was her kidnapper! Next thing you knew, she'd be wielding a machine gun and calling herself Patty Hearst.

"Never had any reason to go back." Another shrug, this one indifferent.

"No family?" Another mental kick in the shin.

He shook his head. "My parents died when I was fifteen."

Despite all common sense, a rush of sympathy slid through her. "That must have been tough." She paused. "How did they die?"

He hesitated for several long seconds, and when he finally spoke, his answer chilled her to the bone. "My father shot my mother in the head before turning the gun on himself. Good old murder-suicide."

Lana gasped. "Oh, God. Why…why did he do it?"

"To this day, I still have no clue." His entire face had darkened, making him appear lethal, unapproachable.

"That must have been awful," she whispered.

"Did you go to live with family? Grandparents? Aunt and uncle?"

Deacon's eyes grew shuttered. "No."

"Then where—"

"Delta! Bring her over here!" came Le Clair's hard shout, officially putting an end to the conversation.

Lana found herself overwhelmed with sadness as she followed Deacon. Her brain reprimanded her for being affected by Deacon's horrifying tale, while her heart wept for the angry, grief-stricken teenage boy who'd lost his parents in such a gruesome way. She fought the urge to squeeze his arm and shifted her focus to Le Clair, who'd walked down the porch steps to meet them.

When Le Clair stuck his cell phone in her direction, all thoughts of Deacon and his painful confession flew out of Lana's head in one fell swoop. "Say hello to your father, princess," Le Clair ordered, "and make it fast."

Joy exploded in Lana's body like a burst of

Fourth of July fireworks. Her father! Oh, thank God, this was finally going to be over!

She grabbed at the phone like a passenger on a sinking ship grasping for a life preserver. "Daddy?" she said urgently.

A hiss of static, and then her father's familiar voice came on the line. "Lana! How are you? *Where* are you?"

Her dad sounded as if he might be fighting tears, and Lana blinked back the moisture seeping from her own eyes. *Think!* she ordered herself. She had to be smart, had to give her dad a clue about where she was.

She let out a wobbly breath and spoke into the mouthpiece, slowly, evenly. "I'm fine, Daddy. I know we haven't always gotten along, but I want you to know that I love you. And on the remote chance that I survive this ordeal, I hope we can elevate our relationship to a higher place—"

"Time's up," Le Clair snapped, and then the phone was snatched out of her hand. Her captor repeated the same warning into the mouthpiece. "Time's up, Kelley. You know what to do."

Le Clair jammed on the disconnect button and shoved the cell phone into the pocket of his impeccable wool trousers. Then he glanced over at Lana with a smirk. "So you and Daddy don't get along, huh, princess?"

Actually, they got along great, but Lana had been grasping at straws. She'd tried revealing her location in the mountains with the words *remote, elevate* and *higher place,* but she had no idea if Hank had picked up on it.

The sound of her father's voice still echoed in her mind. She'd never heard him sound so frantic, so broken-up. He'd always been the smooth-talking senator, but during those precious few seconds, he'd sounded like a worried, heartbroken father. The thought made her sick with anxiety. The rest of her family must be going out of their minds, too.

"He's a hard man to love," she said vaguely, in response to Le Clair's mocking query.

"Can't say I'm surprised," he answered, smirking again. "Your sweet mother must be finding it difficult to love him, too, if what the news stories are saying is true."

Lana had no desire to talk about her parents' marital problems with this son of a bitch. Gritting her teeth, she turned to Deacon. "May I go back to my room now?"

Le Clair let out a laugh. "Ah, I see I hit a nerve. By all means, Delta, take our princess back to her royal chamber."

Deacon led her back inside, and the second they were alone in the bedroom again, he spun around, his hazel eyes flashing with fury. "What the *hell* are you doing, Lana?"

She almost stumbled from the force of his glare. "What are you talking about?"

"'Elevate our relationship to a higher place'?" Deacon made a frustrated noise. "Don't think I didn't pick up on what you were doing, dropping hints to your father."

"I did no such thing," she lied. "I was merely

expressing my regret that Daddy and I don't have a closer relationship."

"Bullshit." The anger in his eyes faded, replaced by a rueful look. "That was risky. You're very lucky Le Clair didn't figure it out."

She offered a tiny shrug. "I don't know what you're talking about."

To her surprise, his mouth twitched, as if he were suppressing a grin. "Whatever you say, *princess.*"

She undid her coat and draped it over the broken chair by the desk, then headed to the bed and sat down cross-legged. Outside, the sun was completely obstructed by thick gray clouds, and the damp breeze drifting in from the open window hinted at impending rain.

She still felt shaken up by the conversation with her father, but she refused to let Deacon see it. Call it a family trait, but Kelleys had been trained from birth not to show weakness. But Lord…her father had sounded so devastated. As tears prickled her eyelids, she blinked a few times, then put on a careless front and raised a brow at Deacon.

"Do you guys have any books out there?" she grumbled. "Or a magazine? You can't expect me to sit here for the rest of my time here doing absolutely nothing. I'll die of boredom."

A strange expression crossed Deacon's face. "Actually, I, uh…" He cleared his throat. "I have something for you."

She tamped down her curiosity as he left the room with brisk strides. Less than a minute later, he reappeared in the doorway, holding a stack of sketching paper, yellowed from age, and a small plastic bag filled with…coal?

"I found this in the living room," he said, sounding awkward as he held up the paper. "And I got the charcoal from the fireplace. I figured you could use it to sketch something, as long as you're here."

The warmth that flooded her chest was incredibly inappropriate. Not to mention infuriating. So what if he'd scrounged up some art supplies? That certainly didn't make up for the fact that he was a willing participant in her *abduction.*

"Thanks," she said woodenly, determined not to let the gesture affect her.

Deacon set the materials on the desk and edged back to the door. "I'll check in on you later," he murmured, and then he was gone.

Lana stared at the closed door, wondering why it was that she softened up whenever Deacon was around. She kept having to remind herself that he had kidnapped her. She wasn't allowed to like the man, not anymore anyway. She wasn't supposed to feel touched that he'd remembered how much she loved art, and that he'd risked facing Le Clair's wrath in order to take her outside.

Yep, she wasn't supposed to do any of that, and yet she was.

"See that, baby," she whispered to the precious life growing inside of her. "Daddy brought us some art supplies." Her tone suddenly hardened. "Now, if he'd just quit being a jerk and let us go, then Mommy will be *really* happy."

Unfortunately, she knew that wasn't going to be an option. No matter how many times Deacon promised he'd protect her, he wouldn't free her. Which meant she was stuck here, at least until her father gave these men what they wanted.

The only problem was, something made her think that money might not be the answer to her problems.

You know what to do.

The words Le Clair had barked at her father floated into the forefront of her brain. What did that mean? What exactly did they want her father to do? Each day that passed here in these isolated mountains brought the ominous suspicion that this entire situation was a lot bigger than money, that she and her father might be caught up in something neither of them was capable of handling.

And that, more than anything that had happened so far, scared her to death.

Chapter 6

By the time the two-week mark of Lana's captivity rolled by, Deacon was growing considerably wary about this job. Two weeks was a long time to keep a hostage. A *very* long time.

He didn't like it one bit.

As he prepared a grilled cheese sandwich for Lana's lunch, he mulled over the situation, wondering if he should approach Le Clair with his concerns. The boss was beginning to look frazzled these days, spending most of his time on the porch mumbling into his cell phone, though to whom he was mumbling was a mystery to Deacon. He got the feeling Le Clair wasn't happy with the way things were going, but Deacon wasn't privy to the details. Was Hank Kelley refusing to pay up?

Deacon's eyebrows knitted together in a frown as he cut the sandwich in half and set it on a chipped yellow dish. He knew Lana was growing frustrated, too, and deeply impatient. He checked on her frequently, and their afternoon walks had become a daily ritual. At first she'd pressed him about his childhood, trying to get more details about his parents' deaths, but she'd eventually given up when he remained vague about it, and proceeded to chatter on aimlessly about her own life. He knew it was her way to get her mind off her current predicament, but Deacon had started clinging to the stories she told.

He felt as though he knew everything about her now. She told him wry anecdotes about her overprotective older brothers, spoke of her parents with deep emotion, raved about art, modestly described some of the sculptures in her recent body of work. The more time he spent with her, the more he liked and respected Lana Kelley. Which was why this assignment was starting to trouble him. He didn't want to see her get hurt, and the way Le Clair angrily muttered into that cell phone of his didn't bode well for Lana.

"Lunch," he said gruffly as he entered the back bedroom.

Lana's head lifted at his arrival. She was sitting cross-legged on the floor, hunched over a sheet of sketching paper. Her long blond hair fell onto her face, and her slender fingers were stained black from the charcoal.

"Thanks," she said absently, her hand moving quickly across the paper, adding details to the face in her sketch.

Deacon was startled when he realized it was *his* face. She was drawing him, and from the looks of it, the likeness was uncanny. Apparently she was very, very good at what she did.

After adding one last smudge underneath his

left eye, she set down the charcoal and stood up, accepting the wet napkin he handed her and scrubbing at the tips of her fingers. Then she picked up the plate and took a bite of the grilled cheese, chewing fervently.

"I'm starving," she said between mouthfuls.

Deacon hid a smile. He glanced at the portrait she'd left lying on the floor, noticed the other papers scattered next to it and realized she'd done a few more sketches. Faces.

He frowned. Tango's sharp mouth and prominent scar glared up at him, while another sheet displayed Le Clair's feral features and thin lips curled in a sneer.

"You're drawing us," he said uneasily.

She chewed slowly, nodding. "It's not like I have any other subjects."

His uneasiness intensified. "Can't you sketch the mountains?"

"I already told you, I do faces. That's what my work is about, bringing interesting faces to life."

Maybe so, but she'd done a lot more than that

here. She'd cataloged each one of her kidnappers, producing accurate sketches that any lawenforcement agency could use to nab each and every one of them. Including Deacon.

Lana gave him a knowing look. "I'll rip them up when I'm done. Don't worry, *Delta,* the cops won't see these." She swallowed the last bite of her sandwich and set the plate down on the desk. "But you will get caught," she added. "You know that, right?"

He didn't respond.

"You guys won't get away with this," she continued, her blue eyes glittering with defiance. "My family will find me."

Her words made his chest squeeze in the most disconcerting way. *You guys.* It sent a streak of agony through him that she associated him with the others. But why shouldn't she? He'd been a full participant in this abduction, and she had every reason to despise him. Yet she didn't seem to.

"Why?" he burst out.

Her forehead wrinkled. "Why will they find me? Because they're—"

"No," he cut in. "Why don't you despise me?"

She fixed him with a sad stare. "Who says I don't?"

His heart twisted. "Do you?"

Her silence tore at his insides like a ravenous scavenger. He didn't know why, but the thought of Lana hating him was almost unbearable. He knew he was the bad guy here, that he'd taken her against her will in order to score a wad of cash, but he didn't want to be the object of this woman's hatred. Lana Kelley was…she was an incredible woman. She'd handled her two-week stint as a hostage with the utmost grace, and the inner strength that radiated from her pores impressed the hell out of him. She was smart, gorgeous, funny when she dropped her guard long enough to loosen up around him. She was a woman he'd be proud to call his own, if he weren't such a cold, lifeless ghost of a human being.

"No."

Lana's quiet voice sliced through his thoughts, making him glance up in shock. "No?" he echoed.

"I don't hate you." She shook her head in be-wilderment. "I should, right? I should want to rip your throat out for what you're doing to me. So why don't I?"

"I have no idea," he admitted hoarsely. "You have every right to hate me."

"Maybe...maybe it's because I don't believe you're one of them." She gestured to the door, as if to point at the men beyond it. "They're all greedy. Heartless. Especially Le Clair. He doesn't seem to care one bit that he's got me locked up in this cabin like a prisoner."

She let out a shaky breath. "But I get the feeling that *you* care." She met his eyes. "Am I crazy? Am I pathetic for believing that? God, for all I know, you're playing me, making me think you actually give a damn, but really—"

"I give a damn," he interjected, stunned by

the slight crack in his voice. "I'm not playing you, Lana." He was embarrassed by the next words that popped almost unconsciously from his mouth. "I've never met anyone like you. That night at the Louvre…it was…"

He trailed off awkwardly, but Lana wouldn't let it go. "It was what?" she said softly.

"It was really nice." He lifted his shoulders, then let them sag. "It was the first time in a long time I felt…at peace."

She bit her bottom lip. "Do you…um, have a girlfriend?"

Her question shocked the hell out of him. "What?"

"I figured I'd ask. I mean, you lied about who you really are, maybe when you told me at the hotel that you were single, you were lying about that, too."

Her words were like an arrow to the heart. Somehow, her complete lack of trust in him made him want to hit something, namely him-self. She might not hate him, but her distrust was just as bad. Still, he knew no amount of time or gestures could ever make her trust him again. She had, that night in Paris, but no more.

"I'm single," he said, his voice rough. "I didn't lie about that."

"Oh." She visibly swallowed. "All right."

"Does it make a difference?" he couldn't help but ask.

She lifted her head and met his gaze head-on, laughing ruefully. "I guess it shouldn't, huh? Here I am, worrying I might have been the other woman, when at the moment, I have plenty of other things to worry about."

As if on cue, the door swung open with such force it banged against the paint-chipped wall and brought a gust of cold air into the room. Le Clair looked annoyed as hell as he marched across the weathered wood floor and thrust the phone into Lana's hands. "Keep it short," he growled at her.

Deacon's entire body went on edge as he watched Lana grab for the phone like a starving child desperate for food. "Dad, it's me," she said quickly. She listened for a moment, and Deacon could see her brain working overtime in that pretty blond head of hers, trying to formulate another clue.

Sure enough, in a cool and composed voice, she said, "I know you were always closer to the capital than you were to your children, but when this is over, I hope we can spend some time together, maybe accept Mr. Bradshaw's offer to—"

"Shut up," Le Clair hissed at her, his gray eyes shooting daggers at Lana, who gasped as he violently snatched the phone and shoved her away.

Deacon stiffened as Lana stumbled backward and nearly fell onto the bed. He forced himself to keep a cool head, listening as Le Clair lifted the phone to his ear and barked, "Time's up. You know what to do if you want her to live."

Lana gasped again, her eyes growing as wide as saucers. She evidently hadn't missed the deadly note in that last sentence. The gasp became a squeak when Le Clair grabbed her shoulders with both hands and shook so hard Deacon could swear he heard Lana's teeth rattle.

"Who the hell is Bradshaw?" Le Clair roared, his French accent becoming more pronounced in his fury. "What were you saying to your father, you little bitch?"

Lana shrank back, but Deacon had to give her credit. She played the part of cowering female to a *T*, her bottom lip quivering, her eyes filling with tears. Only the almost-imperceptible flicker of defiance in her gaze revealed the truth. She was playing Le Clair, and the man had no freaking clue.

Deacon hid a grin.

"Ernie Bradshaw," she whimpered between tiny sobs. "He owns an insurance company, and D-Daddy and I saw h-him a few months ago. He invited us to his s-summer house in Cape Cod. I thought if I reminded Daddy about it, it would lift his s-spirits."

"Next time, you keep it short when I ask you to," Le Clair snapped. "I don't have the patience for pathetic little anecdotes, you understand?"

She nodded quickly. "I'm sorry, I didn't think…"

"Then start thinking! You've got a brain in that pretty head, don't you? Well, use it." The rage on Le Clair's face dimmed slightly, only to ignite as the papers on the floor caught his eye.

All the air in the room went utterly icy. A tense silence hung over the space as Le Clair slowly bent down and picked up the sketches Lana had done of his men. Of himself. Without moving, he stared at the sketches, unblinking, unspeaking.

Deacon took a protective step to the side, toward Lana, but he wasn't quick enough. Before he could move, Le Clair's hands were on the slender blonde again and he shoved her against the wall with incredible force.

"What is *this?*" he boomed, waving the papers in front of her face. "What the *hell* are you doing?"

Tears streamed down Lana's silky cheeks. "They're just drawings," she protested. "I promised I would tear them up when—"

The back of Le Clair's hand came smashing down on her face, making her head slam against the wall. The tears fell harder, and Deacon fought wave after wave of red-hot fury. He was two seconds away from strangling the life right out of Paul Le Clair, when the man abruptly let Lana go, cursing in French beneath his breath.

Le Clair crumpled the drawings with one big hand and shoved them into his pocket. "You want to draw?" he said in a low, menacing voice. "Then draw some flowers or rainbows or puppies and kittens. If I see anything like this again, you won't like the consequences, princess."

As Lana stood there, shuddering and crying softly, Le Clair stormed out of the room.

Deacon stared into Lana's terrified blue eyes,

at her tearstained cheeks, then sighed and followed his boss. He caught up with Le Clair at the end of the dark hallway, clearing his throat to get his attention.

"You gave her this paper?" Le Clair demanded, holding up the crumpled drawings.

"The pictures are harmless, sir. You know I would have destroyed them."

Le Clair paused for a moment, then nodded in resignation. "Yes, I know that. I may have overreacted a tad." He smoothed out the sketch of his own face, studying it carefully. "She's quite good. But it's very disconcerting, seeing your own image staring back at you, isn't it?"

"Yes," Deacon agreed. As Le Clair took a step, Deacon hurriedly added, "Sir..."

"What is it, Delta?"

"I assure you, I'm truly not trying to second-guess your methods here, and I mean no disrespect, but I'm not sure her family will be happy if any harm comes to her." Deacon kept his tone completely neutral, almost humble. "Do you think it was a good idea, striking her?"

For a moment he thought Le Clair would explode again, but the man just sighed. "No, it probably wasn't smart. But I'm having some difficulty with the negotiations." He frowned. "The father is not complying."

Deacon's interested was piqued. "He's refusing to pay?"

"Something like that."

"But surely he's desperate to get his daughter back alive."

Le Clair curled his fist over the drawing, shoving it back into his pocket. "That may not be our end game."

Deacon's interest faded into suspicion. Accompanied by the wild tug of panic at his gut. "You're not planning on returning her to her family?"

Le Clair shrugged.

"Level with me, sir. Who exactly is pulling our strings here?" Deacon pressed.

"That doesn't concern you." Le Clair took a couple of steps, as if he were suddenly eager to get away. "You'll get paid, just as I promised. That's all you need to know for now. Now go check on the princess to make sure she's not too shaken up. We still need her cooperation."

The other man stalked off, leaving Deacon staring after him in growing dismay. *That may not be our end game.* The words brought a deep chill, straight down to the bone. For the first time since he'd accepted this job, Deacon experienced a spark of fear. Was Le Clair planning on killing Lana? Had he never had any intention of letting her go?

Deacon's jaw tensed. He was in this for the money, yes, but he'd agreed to be part of an abduction. Not murder. No, murder had never been on the agenda, and if that was where Le Clair was going with this…well, then Deacon realized he definitely needed to reevaluate.

But first things first—check on Lana and make sure she was okay. The memory of

Le Clair's hand striking her beautiful face made Deacon's insides coil into tight, angry knots. Hopefully Le Clair had learned from the reckless action, and if he hadn't, Deacon knew without a doubt that he wouldn't stand by idly the next time Le Clair decided to take his anger out on Lana.

To his surprise, when he walked into the room, Lana was sitting calmly on the bed. The tears had dried up, and aside from a red mark on her cheek, she looked unharmed.

"Are you okay?" he asked as he closed the door behind him.

"That jerk sure has a temper," she said dryly.

"Le Clair *is* a bit of a hothead," Deacon admitted. He suddenly cocked his head, narrowing his eyes at her. "Who's Bradshaw?"

She gave him an innocent look, like a child who'd just told her parents that Santa was the one who had opened all the presents in the middle of the night. "Exactly who I said he is. The owner of an insurance company and an acquaintance of my dad's."

"And he really owns a house in Cape Cod?"

"How do I know?" She looked quite pleased with herself as she rose from the bed and walked toward him, her arms crossed over her chest. "But he does own a cabin near Sacramento, up in the mountains. Must be pretty close to where we are, no?"

Deacon didn't know whether to kiss her or throttle her. Her intelligence and quick thinking impressed him to no end, but she was playing with fire here, messing with Le Clair. A small part of him disapproved of her cryptic SOSs. He had to think about himself, too. If Lana's clues led her family—and law enforcement—to this cabin, Deacon would be arrested along with the others. And his own self-preservation was extremely important to him.

Still, he couldn't stop the warmth and satisfaction that coursed through him when he thought about what Lana had done.

He met her eyes, and saw the laughter dancing in them. "You can't decide if you should be angry with me or applaud me, right?" she said, sounding delighted.

"Actually, I was torn between throttling you and kissing you." His throat went dry the second the words left his mouth. Crap. Why had he said that? The idea of kissing him ever again probably made her sick to her stomach.

And yet...

At the word *kissing* he heard her breath hitch. And she leaned in closer. He wondered if she even realized she'd done that.

Their gazes locked again, and what he saw on her face stole his breath. She looked as she had the night in his hotel. Cheeks flushed to a rosy pink. Lips slightly parted. The memory of how soft those lips had felt pressed against his own had him moving closer, too, despite every warning bell going off in his head.

It was hard to breathe. Or think. Yeah, he really wasn't thinking as his head dipped ever so slightly. His body went tighter than a drum, taut with anticipation.

His pulse raced.

Her eyes glimmered with reluctant heat.

Their heads moved closer, their lips mere inches apart. The scent of her hair drifted into his nostrils, sweet and feminine and so very addictive. He breathed her in, drowning in the scent, while his body hummed eagerly and his mouth tingled with the need to taste her.

So he did.

Chapter 7

Lana's heart was beating a million times a minute as Deacon's mouth covered hers. Her disloyal body melted against him like butter on a sizzling pan. He smelled so unbelievably good, spicy and masculine, and she couldn't think straight surrounded by that intoxicating scent. And his mouth…it was warm and firm. Familiar. She found herself responding to the kiss, brushing her lips over his even as her brain screamed for her to pull away.

God help her, but she couldn't move. The attraction she'd felt for this man a month ago came crashing back in full force, sending streaks of heat through her body and making every inch of her tingle. As his hands slid down to her waist and moved in a featherlight caress, she was reminded of the slow caresses and lazy kisses he'd bestowed upon her body the night in the hotel.

The night they'd conceived this baby.

She broke off the kiss at that sudden reminder, stumbling backward and sucking in a gulp of air to try and clear her head. "You…you should go," she squeezed out, as her heart thudded relentlessly against her rib cage.

Something that resembled dismay flashed across his rugged face. When Lana glanced south, she noticed the thick hard length of him straining against the zipper of his black pants. His obvious arousal only made her heart beat faster. Lana wanted to kick herself for it.

"I'm sorry," he said hoarsely. He edged toward the door like a stray dog wary of strangers. "I… shouldn't have done that. I'm sorry."

A third mumbled apology and he was out the door. The click of the lock was like the final touch to a ghastly drawing. She'd kissed him. *Kissed* her *abductor*.

Lana's body felt ravaged, hot and needy and tingling with residual desire. The reaction horrified her, had her staggering toward the bed and collapsing on the hard mattress.

"Your mommy is out of her mind," she whispered to her belly. "This ordeal has obviously messed your mom up, big-time."

Her tiny son or daughter didn't respond, of course, but Lana could swear she felt a ripple of movement in her womb. Her brain told her it was impossible; she was only four weeks along. Babies didn't start kicking until, what? Sixteen, seventeen weeks? But the phantom flutter succeeded in calming her down. Her pulse slowed to a regular rhythm, and her chest, seconds ago tight with shock and desire, loosened considerably.

"Okay, this isn't so terrible," she said. "Mommy and Daddy kissed. No big deal."

But it *was* a big deal. Deacon Holt had lied

to her, seduced her and kidnapped her. She wasn't supposed to have any feelings for the man. None. Zilch. Zero.

Yet for some reason, she still couldn't lump him into the same evil category as the others. Her instincts had never failed her before, and right now, they were telling her that deep down, Deacon Holt was a good man.

Was she crazy to think that?

Several hours later, she got the answer to that question when Deacon entered the back room with stiff robotic movements, a dinner tray in his hands. He barely looked in her direction as he held out the tray. Steam rose from the plate, carrying the aroma of grilled chicken and roasted potatoes. It smelled so good her mouth watered involuntarily.

If there was one good thing about this ordeal—and good was a real stretch here—it was the food. Sure beat the bland pasta dishes she cooked up for herself back in her Florence apartment. She took after her mom—couldn't cook worth a damn. Her aunt Bonnie Gene was a whiz in the kitchen, though. Lana always looked forward to Bonnie Gene's yummy home-cooked meals whenever she visited her brother Cole in Maple Cove, Montana.

Accepting the tray, Lana slid back so she was leaning against the wall. She picked up the plastic fork, then hesitated. "Who's doing the cooking?" she couldn't help but ask.

"Me."

Her head lifted in surprise. "Really?" When he nodded in confirmation, she said, "How'd you learn to cook so well?"

His response came in the form of a shrug.

"Do you like it?" Okay, she was totally grasping at straws here, but making idle conversation was the only way to ensure she didn't bring up that explosive kiss.

Obviously, it wasn't even on his mind, which meant she needed to follow his lead and pretend it hadn't happened. Pretend that she hadn't kissed her kidnapper. Hadn't brushed her mouth against his, or parted her lips in anticipation, longing for the taste of his tongue.

"Are we going to talk about this?" she blurted out.

Wonderful. So much for pretending it never happened.

"What's there to talk about?" Deacon's tone was indifferent, almost cold, and it totally grated on her nerves.

"We kissed," she said, her stern voice reminding her of the tone her brother Cole's housekeeper, Hannah, used to reprimand her when she stole cookies off the baking sheet.

"It was a mistake."

Lana raised a brow. "That's it? That's all you have to say about it?"

"Uh-huh."

He was already edging for the door. Lana got the feeling he did that a lot. Cut and ran whenever things got too uncomfortable for him.

"Do you feel anything, ever?" she found herself grumbling. "Or do you always act like a lifeless robot around women?"

He didn't even blink. Didn't answer, either, which intensified her frustration.

"Why are you like this?" she burst out. "I know you're not a robot, Deacon. That night in the hotel, you were...*alive.* You laughed and joked and teased me. You were passionate and gentle and..." Her voice trailed. She felt as though she was talking to a brick wall.

"An aberration," he finally said, a sigh seeping from his massive chest. "Those words you just used—*passionate, gentle.* That's not me, Lana."

"Then who are you, damn it?" She kept her voice low, but every fiber of her being wanted to shout at this man.

"I'm the man who kidnapped you for money."

His words were harsh, brooking no argument, seeking no acceptance. She stared at his handsome face, that big, lean body. His eyes had darkened to a forest green, and for the first time since they'd met, Lana saw something in his gaze. It was a tiny, almost indiscernible flicker, but she recognized it instantly.

Shame.

He was ashamed.

But of what? His part in her abduction? Past actions? Or was he ashamed of himself? Of who he was, on a cellular level?

"When I was twelve, my brother Dylan dated this girl…Mandy," Lana started softly. "Everyone in my family adored her. She was a pretty brunette, smart, great sense of humor. She treated my parents like royalty, always helping clean up after dinner even though we had three housekeepers to do it. She helped me with my homework. Brought little thoughtful gifts for my mom, talked politics with my dad. She was totally perfect."

Deacon eyed her warily. "Why are you telling me this?"

"Just…listen." She took a breath. "So she was perfect, right, but no matter how hard I tried, I always got this nagging little feeling when she was around. She didn't do a thing to warrant my suspicions, but they were there."

Deacon quit moving toward the door, growing still and silent as he listened. "And were you right to be suspicious?"

Lana nodded. "Turned out she was stealing from us. Jewelry, family heirlooms, pieces of silver, even random knickknacks. Mom ended up firing one of our housekeepers—Mandy had planted a necklace in the woman's room when my parents started noticing the thefts. When the truth came out, everyone was shocked."

"But not you."

"Not me." She set the dinner tray beside her on the bedspread, her hunger forgotten. Leaning forward, she clasped her hands in her lap and met his eyes. "I get feelings about people. I've had them since I was a little girl. I know, without reason or provocation, whether someone is a good person or a truly vile one. I knew it about Mandy, when there wasn't a single sign to prove otherwise." She took a breath. "And I sense it about you."

He spoke in a pained voice. "That I'm vile?"

"That you're the opposite," she said with the shake of her head. "Deep down, I think you're a good man."

Disbelief filled his eyes. "Good?" he balked. "I'm sorry to burst your bubble, sweetheart, but there's nothing good about me. As I just pointed out, I'm a willing party in your kidnapping."

A tornado of despair swirled in her stomach. He kept reminding her of that, and yet she kept disregarding it. What was wrong with her? Why was she determined to cling to the notion that Deacon Holt was a good person?

"I think," he began slowly, "that for once, your sixth sense has failed you." He sighed. "Actually, I don't think it's a sixth sense at all, Lana. Maybe with your brother's girlfriend, but right here, right now, it's plain old idealism that's making you see things that aren't there."

"I'm not idealistic," she whispered.

"Yes, you are." His mouth twisted ruefully. "Maybe it's because you're an artist, or maybe you've just never had anything bad happen to you. But you seek perfection where it doesn't exist, Lana."

"No."

"Yes." He gave a bleak laugh. "In fact, you remind me of myself, when I was younger. I was optimistic, too, once, before reality crashed in. A word of advice, sweetheart, you can't cling to fantasy forever. Eventually reality will settle in."

She clamped her teeth over her lower lip. The bitterness in his voice was so thick she felt it in the air. God, the things he must have experienced in his life, awful, tragic things that had turned him into a man who believed nothing good existed—in the world, or in him.

But...

But was he right? Was she grabbing at anything here in her need to excuse Deacon's actions because he was the father of her child?

Their child. Maybe this was the time to tell him. The only concrete way to find out if her confidence in the man was sound.

If he knew, would he let her go? Or would he prove her instincts wrong and continue to keep her here against her will?

Releasing a breath, Lana raised her head to meet his gaze. She had to tell him. Now. She *had* to.

"Deacon," she started. "I—"

"You're wrong about me," he interrupted. "I'm not good. There is nothing, absolutely nothing, decent about me. You don't want or need someone like me in your life, and once this is all over, I'll be gone. We'll never see each other again."

Disappointment floated into her chest. Her mouth closed. The temptation to tell him about the baby still remained strong, but she suddenly knew he wasn't ready to hear it. Something had happened to this man. Maybe it was the death of his parents, or maybe some other traumatic event had skewed his entire outlook. Whatever it was, it had broken him beyond repair. Hearing he was going to be a father would not fix it. Not now anyway.

"So don't worry, very soon I'll be out of your life forever," he finished roughly.

Without waiting for an answer or an objection, he left the room. Lana drew in a breath, slightly stunned by the passionate way he'd recited that dismal speech. He truly believed he was a bad person. And heck, maybe he was right. Maybe her sixth sense *was* steering her in the wrong direction.

But he'd been wrong about one thing. He would never be out of her life forever. A part of him would always remain in her life—their child.

You have to tell him.

She sighed. Yes, she knew Deacon needed to hear the truth, even if the truth changed nothing between them.

Soon, she vowed. She would tell him soon.

* * *

Sarah had never liked the Atlantic Ocean. It was too cold, too unpredictable. As she walked the shoreline in front of Vivienne's beach house, she looked at the choppy waves and shivered. Despite the fact that the ship had gone down miles and miles from here, she could almost imagine the ghosts from the *Titanic* lurking beneath those waves, sobbing with grief and agony.

She felt like sobbing, too, right about now. A month. An entire damned month had passed since her daughter had been taken prisoner, and she was going crazy with worry. Hank had been calling with weekly updates, but he never had anything useful to say, save for the fact that he was "working on it."

Working on what? She wanted her daughter home, safe and sound. And she wanted it *now.* As far as the professors at the university knew, Lana was visiting her brother in Montana, and the faculty hadn't questioned it, which meant the media had no idea Lana was even missing. That was another reason Hank wanted to keep the police out of it, as filing an official report meant the press would immediately get wind of the situation. That had been fine by her—two weeks ago. Now she just wanted to call every media outlet out there in hopes that plastering Lana's face all over the world would provide them with a lead, but Hank had convinced her to stay silent. For now.

If something wasn't done, though—and soon—Sarah had already decided to take matters into her own hands.

As if on cue, her cell phone began to ring. She fumbled in the pocket of the long cardigan sweater she'd thrown on before coming outside. Whipping the phone to her ear, she said, "Have you found her?"

Hank's voice was strained. "Not yet, but I think we've figured out where she's being held."

Hope soared through her. "Where?" she demanded.

"In the mountains, north of Sacramento. Remember those clues I told you about, the words she spoke during the calls? Well, my bodyguard Gage figured out where they must be keeping her."

"Did you inform the FBI?"

Silence greeted her ears.

"Damn it, Hank! You didn't call them, did you?"

He sounded guarded as he said, "There are things at work here that you don't understand, darling. I'm doing my best."

Right, because his *best* had always served them well in the past. Sarah almost wished her husband were standing in front of her, so she could strangle him. She'd heard from her son Dylan that one of Hank's mistresses had attacked him in Maple Cove, but even now—or maybe especially now—she couldn't muster up any concern or sympathy. Hank Kelley deserved what he got.

"I'm going to call Jim," she said decisively, referring to their youngest son, who was currently on an overseas assignment with his Special Forces unit.

"No." Hank's tone brooked no argument. "Leave the boy out of this. I've already sent someone to get Lana."

She faltered. "Who did you send?"

"A mercenary, one of the best in the world." Encouragement rang from the other end of the line. "He's going to find her, Sarah, and he's going to bring her home safely. I promise you that."

She drew in a long breath, fixing her gaze on the dark water ahead. "Okay," she said, her voice soft and lacking the confidence her husband seemed to be feeling. "Just get our baby home, Hank. Please."

"I will," he vowed.

Sarah ended the connection and tucked the phone into her pocket. Then she wrapped her arms around her chest and slowly walked back to the house.

* * *

Okay, so *soon* was a relative term, Lana decided after two more weeks had passed and the truth about the baby had yet to reach Deacon's ears. But she'd *tried.* Each time he came into the room brandishing another delicious meal, she came close to revealing the pregnancy. Once, she'd even babbled on about what a lively baby she'd been, hoping it would provide a smooth interlude into "maybe the baby we're having will be lively, too."

But the words refused to reach the surface, and Deacon's gruff, aloof demeanor hadn't helped any. He'd shut down on her again. Ever since the kiss, he kept her at arm's length. The afternoon walks continued, but they lacked any and all discussion. She'd run out of stories to tell him, so now they walked in silence, while Le Clair fumed on the porch—when he wasn't taking off for days at a time.

Le Clair's frequent absences had begun to

worry Lana. What was going on in the real world? Why was she still *here?*

It pained her to admit it, but evidently the clues she'd tried giving her father had gone unnoticed. Somehow she doubted her family was up in a helicopter searching these mountains. She would've heard the whir of rotors overhead, and besides, it wouldn't take two weeks to comb the entire area. There were only a handful of accessible locations near Sacramento, which meant that her father hadn't picked up on the word *capital* and if he had, he hadn't connected it with California.

She'd been a prisoner for more than a month, and with each day that passed, hope began slipping away. She tried clinging to it, squeezing it between her fingers before she lost it completely, but every hour, every minute, scissors of fear hacked away at that ribbon of hope.

"I'm going to die here," she whispered into the darkness.

The sun had just set, and Deacon had already

taken away her dinner tray. That meant she got to spend the rest of the night in this room, alone. The papers and charcoal were abandoned on the desk. She'd given up on sketching days ago, no longer able to muster up any creativity.

Her voice cracked as she spoke to her unborn child. "Oh, baby, what are we going to do?"

Tears stuck to her lashes, then broke free and streamed down her cheeks, leaving watery trails on her skin. She was pregnant and alone and so far away from her family, in emotional distance at least. She missed them all desperately, even more than when she'd been away at school.

"I'm scared." The two syllables slipped through her lips, the terror and misery they resonated hanging in the dark room like a relentless fog.

She tried not to show that fear when Deacon was around, but he must be picking up on it by now. If he only knew how deep the fear truly ran. Already, her body had begun to show the signs of her condition. Her breasts were growing fuller, and they ached all the time now. Her belly was still flat, but how much longer would it remain that way? A month? Two? A tremor of distress ran through her. When a baby bump made an appearance, she'd have no way of keeping the truth from Deacon. She'd made a show of taking a tampon out of her toiletry case, under the pretense that she was on her cycle, but soon she wouldn't be able to fool him.

Lana wiped away her tears, soaking the sleeve of her flannel shirt. It was one of the shirts her captors had purchased for her, serving as another reminder that she had zero control over her own life. She was trapped, a caged animal at the mercy of its handlers. She depended on them for food, shelter, warmth. Supervised walks. Locked door. She didn't even know what day it was anymore. Definitely mid-October by now, but what was the date? Her uncle Donald's birthday was on the fourteenth. Had she missed it? Had her family flown to Montana as they always did? Her father, probably not. He and

Don had been estranged for years, and Hank Kelley made no effort to be cordial to his brother.

But what about Mom? Dylan? Had they celebrated the occasion on Cole's ranch? Was Jim on an assignment? Had Jake returned from his?

So many questions, and not a single answer. All she knew was that she wasn't sure how much longer she could stand this.

"No," she said aloud, her hand curling protectively over her belly. "Your mommy will stand it for as long as she needs to. Nothing is going to happen to you, baby. I promise."

Her blood hummed with a sudden rush of strength. She refused to give in to this hopelessness. She was a Kelley. She came from a long line of strong, confident women capable of surviving anything in their path. This was just a minor hiccup, a rocky obstacle in the road.

"I *will* overcome this," she whispered with the lift of her chin.

As if a higher power had decided to applaud

her fortitude, a gust of wind shook the window. Lana jumped, her pulse speeding up then slowing as she laughed in the darkness. "Just the wind," she soothed, rubbing her tummy. "Mommy's being jumpy."

But then the window rattled again, and this time, the speedy kick of her pulse had nothing to do with fear. There was someone out there! Someone outside the window, signaling to get her attention.

Deacon? Had he finally decided to get her out of here?

Lana stumbled off the bed and bounded to the window, her blond hair falling into her eyes. She shoved the errant strands away and focused on the dirty windowpane.

Her heart nearly stopped when a shadowy face appeared in front of the glass.

Lana sucked in her breath. It wasn't Deacon, that much she could tell. The man on the other side of the window had a goatee circling his mouth. The moment their gazes locked, the stranger raised his finger to his lips, urging her to remain silent, but Lana's throat was so tight with emotion she wouldn't have been able to make a sound anyway.

She was being rescued!

Chapter 8

Lana's body was riddled with impatience as her savior took his sweet time liberating her from the cabin. As she watched, he removed a small silver tool from the belt around his trim waist. A glass cutter, she realized. While her heart beat up a storm, she resisted tapping her foot as he dragged the cutter against the edges of the window. He worked slowly, dark brows drawn together in meticulous concentration.

Who was he? Obviously some kind of soldier, judging from the camo outfit he had on, the black wool hat and the endless supply of tools clipped to his belt. Not to mention the rifle.

She suddenly wondered if he'd used the thing in order to get this close to the cabin. A spark of worry ignited in her stomach. Charlie and the others usually walked the perimeter and stood guard, but Deacon hadn't been back to this room in several hours. What if he'd been assigned to watch the cabin, and had encountered this man outside?

She pushed away the troubling thought. With extreme skill, the man removed the glass, then disappeared from view as he set it down on the ground. He popped up a second later, and for the first time in a month, Lana heard a voice that didn't belong to Deacon or her captors.

"Lana Kelley?" he said, his voice barely above a whisper.

She nodded urgently.

"I'm Rick Garrison." He tucked the glass cutter back in his belt. "Your father sent me."

Relief soared inside her. "Thank God."

"Are you hurt?" Garrison asked. "Can you walk?"

"I'm fine. Please, just get me out of here."

"Do you have a coat?"

She noticed then that his breath left puffs of white in the air. A chill swept into the room, making her turn to the chair where she'd draped her coat. "It's bright red," she told him. "Will that be a problem?"

Garrison nodded briskly, already removing his own fitted black jacket. "Put this on," he ordered, handing her the coat through the empty square left in the window.

She took it and quickly shoved her arms into the sleeves without bothering to zip up the coat. Then she climbed onto the small desk, biting her lip when the wood squeaked from the added weight. She glanced toward the door. Nobody came. Turning back to the window, she leaned forward, then hesitated when a thought occurred to her. Hadn't Deacon said there was a motion sensor on her window?

Yes, he *had* said that.

"Motion sensor," she blurted out, feeling panicked as she looked at Garrison.

"Taken care of," was all he said. "Come on
now. We need to hurry."

Adrenaline spiked in her blood. Lana went out
head-first, landing in Garrison's arm with the
grace of a tourist. He steadied her, his dark eyes
sweeping across her face to assess her well-
being.

"They didn't hurt you?" he said quietly.

She shook her head.

"Your father will be happy to hear that."
Garrison removed a lethal-looking pistol from
his waistband. "Do you know how to use this?"

"Y-yes. My brothers took me to the shooting
range a few times."

Garrison's fingers were warm as he gently
placed the weapon in her hand. He unslung his
rifle from his shoulder, holding it with complete ease. "You're going to have to be extremely quiet. And very quick. I came here by
foot, through the mountains, but I managed to

leave an ATV up on the trail, about five miles from here. Can you handle that?"

Five miles. Lana tried not to cringe. She wasn't out of shape by any means, but a five-mile hike in this bitter cold was not going to be pleasant. Still, she was determined to keep up. "I can handle it," she said grimly.

"See that cluster of rocks?" Garrison gestured to a spot about a hundred yards away.

Lana nodded.

"That's where we need to be." He grimaced. "If I tell you to run, you run, all right? I've been up in the mountains for days, watching the cabin, and I've gotta tell you, these bastards are pros. They don't have a recognizable routine."

"Isn't that good? Professionals usually know what they're doing," she said feebly. "This could mean they're amateurs."

"There's nothing amateur about the way they've handled this. Uneven shifts, random perimeter checks. Different men each time. They're smart, made sure that anyone who tried to infiltrate wouldn't be able to rely on a clockwork rotation. Which means that the moment we head for those rocks, one of them could be coming out of nowhere."

Lana swallowed. "Okay."

"Now, I took out two of them, but—"

Her heart lodged in her throat. He *killed* two men? Terror jolted through her. What if Deacon was one of them? She told herself she was simply concerned about her baby's father, but deep down she knew there was much, much more to the turbulent wave of fear crashing inside her.

She wanted to ask him to describe the men, but Rick was still talking. "There are still two more walking the perimeter. We need to move, and fast. Are you ready?"

She drew in a breath, releasing it in a visible cloud that drifted in the air. "I'm ready."

"Good. Let's go."

Garrison's eyes moved across the empty clearing in a sharp sweep. They had the cover of darkness on their side, but Lana didn't feel invisible. When Rick gripped her arm and pulled her forward, she followed him blindly. Her pulse raced. The gun in her hand felt out of place. She hoped she didn't have to use it. As their boots crunched against the grass, she cringed, frightened the noise would alert one of her captors, but nobody came after them.

Ten yards. Twenty. She ran alongside Rick Garrison, as the harsh wind slapped her face and whipped her hair around. She spat the long tresses from her eyes and mouth, wishing she'd tied them back in a ponytail, but there'd been no time. As she and Garrison moved in swift, long strides, she couldn't help but glance back at the cabin.

Remorse gathered inside her. Should she have tried to warn Deacon? If Rick Garrison had found the cabin, the authorities were probably on their way, too. He must have contacted them, right?

She pictured metal handcuffs being snapped around Deacon's strong wrists and fought a wave of panic. How would she ever explain to her family that the father of her child was a kidnapper? How would she tell her child that his father was in jail? Or dead. Lord, Deacon could already be dead, if he'd been one of the men Rick "took out."

Worry about that later. Right now, run!

She kept moving, determined to make it to those darn rocks, but she and Rick were five yards short of their destination when the entire clearing was illuminated by bright light.

Lana blinked from the sudden flash, horror spiraling up her chest as she heard angry male voices boom from behind them. Enormous security lights had been installed in the trees. She and Rick were completely visible now, like two prisoners caught in a spotlight while attempting a prison break.

"Don't move!" someone roared.

She froze. Rick's hand was still on her arm, pulling her forward, but then the crack of a rifle exploded in the night air, and he finally came to a reluctant halt, mumbling a stream of curses under his breath.

"Turn around!"

Le Clair's voice this time, and Lana felt like a disobedient child as she slowly turned to face her captors. Next to her, Rick had raised his rifle. She followed his lead, lifting the handgun and aiming it at Le Clair, but her hand shook wildly.

There were about twenty yards separating them from her kidnappers. Rick stood protectively by her side. Across the clearing, Le Clair, Echo and Tango had their weapons trained on the duo. Kilo was off to the left, a rifle perched on his enormous shoulder. Oscar, the silent one who'd bought her all those things from town, was a few feet from Kilo, also holding a rifle. But where was Deacon?

Her breathing quickened, then relaxed when she spotted Deacon at Le Clair's right side, the sleek metal of his gun glimmering in the lights bathing the yard. He was alive. Relief coursed through her, then faded abruptly when she realized just how volatile this situation had become.

It was like a Wild West standoff. Next to her, Rick didn't even blink. Across from them, the five men were equally still.

"Hand the girl over," Le Clair ordered, his weapon trained on Garrison. "Hand her over, and we won't kill you."

"What do we do?" Lana whispered in desperation.

"Shhh." Rick didn't even look at her. Holding his rifle with steady hands, he tossed out his own suggestion. "Let us walk away, and I won't kill *you.*"

Le Clair's laugh reverberated in the clearing, bouncing off the massive trunks of the redwood trees. "My, my, aren't we confident. Five against one, and still so sure of yourself."

"I'm a trained sharpshooter," Rick called back carelessly. "I can take all five of you out in less than ten seconds."

"Yeah, but then you'd have a dead princess

on your hands," Le Clair replied. "Because the second one of us goes down, the others have orders to shoot the hostage. Standard operating procedure, my friend."

"Is that actually standard procedure?" Lana hissed.

Rick shook his head. "In this psycho's world, maybe." He went quiet, his brows knitting together in thought. "I can take them out. If you hit the deck before I take the first shot, I can get 'em all."

His confidence did nothing to soothe her. He'd said so himself—these men were pros. What if she didn't go down fast enough? What if she got hit?

What if she *lost the baby?*

"No," she choked out.

Garrison had already raised his rifle. "When I say the word—"

"*No*. It's too risky!"

"I don't have all night," Le Clair shouted. "Give us the girl and you're free to go."

Rick had Le Clair in his sights. "Not going to happen, *my friend.*"

"Rick, please," she pleaded. "Don't shoot at them."

"On the count of three, hit the ground, Miss Kelley."

"They'll let you go if you give me up," she burst out. "If you do this, we'll both get killed."

"*One.*"

"Hand her over," Le Clair demanded, sounding increasingly annoyed.

Her heart was beating so fast she was surprised it didn't rip through her chest. "Rick, please."

"*Two.*"

Her kidnappers shifted their weapons. Trained them on *her.*

Oh, God. She and Rick would both be killed if he went ahead with this suicidal plan. If it was just her, she might be willing to take her chances, but no way was she going to be responsible for Rick's death. And no way in *hell* was she putting her unborn child at risk.

She glanced at Rick, saw his mouth open, saw his lips begin to form the number three.

Without pausing to analyze her actions, Lana threw herself in front of Garrison's rifle and shouted, "Stop! I'll come back!"

Deacon's heart jammed in his throat as he watched Lana dive in front of the mercenary's rifle. Terror pummeled into him like angry fists, making his gun shake in his hand. What the *hell* was she thinking? The damn woman was going to get herself shot!

When the silent alarm had gone off, Deacon had figured one of the other men had screwed up, maybe tripped a wire. But when he and Echo had been sent to investigate and discovered the bodies of Charlie and Yankee up in the hills, he'd realized this was no error. Charlie or Yankee must have triggered the panic button on their radios before getting their necks snapped, and now the entire situation had erupted in chaos.

"Please!" Lana was shouting, her blue eyes imploring Le Clair. "Nobody has to shoot anybody!"

Deacon could hear the faint muttering of the mercenary who'd nearly aided in Lana's escape, but she ignored the man behind her. "I'm going to lay my gun down," she said, her voice shaking in the cold night air. "And I'm going to walk over to you, all right? Everyone just put down their guns before someone gets hurt."

Le Clair chuckled softly. The sound sent a chill through Deacon's body. Lana was dead wrong. Someone *was* going to get hurt. And the moment she was back in Le Clair's clutches, Lana would realize the price of her sacrifice.

"Sounds fair," Le Clair called. "Walk over to us nice and slow, princess."

Deacon's pulse drummed in his ears as Lana placed the handgun down on the grass. The man beside her still had his weapon trained on them.

The dark hair on his upper lip curled downward as he frowned in frustration. But there was no stopping Lana. Deacon experienced an odd sense of pride, watching Lana walk across the brightly lit clearing. Her shoulders were held high, her refined features hard with determination.

"See, here I am," she said calmly as she reached the men. "Just let him go like you promised."

The moment she joined the group, Tango had an iron grip on her arm, keeping her in place. Without even blinking, Le Clair nodded at Kilo and murmured, "Do it."

The deafening report of a rifle cracked in the air, followed by a soft thud as the man across the clearing slumped down to the ground, a bullet hole between the eyes.

Lana screamed in horror, the piercing sound cutting through Deacon like a hot, sharp blade. She shrugged out of Tango's grasp, trying to hurtle toward the lifeless body lying twenty yards away. Tango yanked violently on her arm, forcing her to stay put.

With tears streaming down her cheeks, Lana spun around to shout at Le Clair. "You promised! You said you'd let him go if I came back!"

"I lied," he said with a smirk.

Before anyone could stop her, Lana launched herself at Le Clair and started beating at his chest with small fists. "You bastard! You just killed a good man, you sick, twisted maniac!"

Le Clair laughed in delight, letting her pound at him with her fists. She was strong for her size, but Le Clair was stronger and bigger, and it was obvious her attack didn't cause him an ounce of pain. Instead, it only seemed to amuse him further. His chest rumbled with laughter, the amusement pouring out of him making Deacon ill.

Le Clair let her go at him for a couple of more seconds, then stepped back with a bored expression. "Do you feel better?" he asked congenially.

Lana slowly let her arms drop to her sides. She was sobbing softly. "You're evil," she whispered, her blue eyes drifting in the direction of her almost-savior's body.

"I've been called worse." With a shrug, Le Clair glanced at Echo and Kilo. "Take care of the body. Let's send our friend back where he came from." A withering glance at Lana, then a sharp order to Deacon. "Get her back to the room. And try and calm our little princess down, will you?"

Nodding in assent, Deacon took hold of Lana's arms and forcibly dragged her back inside. She was shaking so hard his own body was vibrating. Damn it. He recognized the signs of shock when he saw them. Lana's blue eyes had become glazed, her face paler than the snow capping the mountains out in the distance and her shuddering was uncontrollable.

"Oh, God," she said over and over again, her voice coming out in rapid gasps. "I killed him."

Deacon's heart twisted in his chest. He forced

himself to keep walking, now practically carrying her forward with his hands on her waist. She was so tiny, so fragile. He wanted to murder Paul Le Clair for making Lana witness a man's cold-blooded execution.

In the bedroom, he set Lana down on the bed, where she immediately curled on her side, her cheeks stained with moisture, her voice dull as she kept mumbling to herself. "I killed him. Oh, God, I *killed* him."

Deacon sat beside her. He awkwardly placed a comforting hand on her lower back. She jerked abruptly, wiggling away from his hand. "He said he would let him go! How could he say that?" Sobs racked her slender body. She curled into herself tighter, bringing her knees to her chest. "God, Deacon!"

At least she knew he was with her. That was a good sign. She hadn't completely gone off the deep end yet.

He reached for her again. "Lana—"

"I killed him!"

Deacon propelled into action, hauling her balled-up body and lifting it into his lap. He wrapped one arm around her trembling shoulders, stroked her cheek with his other hand. "You didn't kill him, sweetheart."

"Yes I did," she mumbled, the tears pouring down her cheeks.

"Hey. Hey!" He grasped her chin with his fingers and yanked it up. "Look at me. *Look* at me."

Her gaze reluctantly focused on his.

Deacon kept his voice low and even. "You did not kill that man, Lana. He knew the risk he was taking when he showed up here."

"To rescue me! This is my fault, Deacon. My fault! Oh, God…"

Her sobs returned and she buried her face against his chest, soaking the front of his sweater. Deacon held her tightly, letting her cry and shake in his arms. Something shifted in his chest, moved and cracked and made his heart ache. Just when he gave up on deciphering the strange reaction, his chest squeezed and then a dam broke inside of it. Pure, raw emotion filled his body, clogging his throat, tangling in his gut.

He nearly pushed Lana out of his arms. The shock was so immense, so paralyzing, he could barely breathe. He was feeling things he'd thought himself incapable of. Worry. Tenderness. Fear. Desire. And thrown into the mix, something hot and painful, something he'd never experienced before.

What was happening to him?

Better question, what was happening to *Lana?*

As he tried sifting through the kaleidoscope of emotions suddenly spinning through him, Lana lifted her head and practically glued her mouth to his.

A groan lodged in his chest. Her lips were soft, slightly cold from her foray into the chilled night and wet from her tears. And the kiss was almost violent. He was helpless to stop it, latching his mouth to hers, letting her tongue slide through his lips. It was a far cry from the kisses they'd shared in the hotel room. Their noses bumped, teeth clashed, tongues fought a wild, desperate battle for domination.

"Lana—" he choked out, the sound of her name vibrating against their lips.

She didn't answer. Just kissed him again, while the tears continued to slide down her cheeks and stain his face.

And then she took off her shirt.

Chapter 9

Lana Kelley had transformed into a lust-crazed temptress right before Deacon's eyes. Deep down he knew this had nothing to do with lust, or even desire. She was desperate to erase the memory of what had happened outside the cabin. She was still in shock. Completely beside herself with grief. So beyond the concept of thinking clearly.

But like an ass, he didn't stop her.

Truth was, he *needed* this. Just one more time. The halo of integrity and optimism that surrounded her like a ray of pure light had been so addictive the night at the hotel. For a short, incredible time, that light had warmed him, enveloped him. It managed to seep into the darkness inside him, just for a little while, and even now, he could remember how astonishing that felt. To be someone else for a brief period of time. Someone that Lana Kelley wanted to be with. A man worthy of her.

His heart thudded like crazy as he dared to look at her. She wore a black lace bra that hugged her breasts…which looked fuller than he remembered. Deacon didn't pause to question what must have been an original error of perspective, because suddenly Lana was back in his lap, and her mouth sought his out like a heat-seeking missile.

She burrowed against him, parted his thighs with her knees, and then she pressed herself directly on his groin. Her lower body ground against his in a wild, reckless rhythm that threatened every ounce of his quickly crumbling control.

He fell onto his back, mad with arousal and

unable to stop his hands from cupping those mouth-watering breasts over her bra. He squeezed, drawing a soft desperate moan from her lush pink lips.

"Please," she whimpered.

Please, what? Stop? Keep going? Her intentions became clear when her hand slid between them and rubbed the hard ridge of his arousal. His erection jerked from the sudden attention, making Deacon groan quietly.

He thrust a hand to the back of her neck, angling her head so he could deepen the kiss, while his other hand continued stroking her breasts. He slipped a finger under one cup of her lacy bra and caressed her nipple. It hardened under his touch, and he rolled the tiny bud between two fingers, eliciting another moan from Lana.

His control continued to wither away. He couldn't breathe, couldn't focus on anything except the feel of Lana's warm body straddling him, the sweet and eager swirls of her tongue as she nearly devoured his mouth with hot, breathless kisses.

He was on fire. Just like the night in the hotel, he was powerless to stop the heat shooting through him, the rigid set of his muscles, tight with anticipation. He *craved* this woman, his need for her so fierce and shattering he didn't know what to make of it.

But it made him uneasy enough to pull away.

"We can't do this," he said hoarsely.

Lana blinked. Her lips were moist, parted sexily, and her breasts still filled his palms. "What…" She blinked again, and then, as if snapping out of a trance, she scrambled off his lap.

"Oh, my God," she blurted as she fumbled around on the bedspread for the sweater she'd discarded. "What am I doing?"

He was asking himself the same question. He was thirty-eight years old, for Pete's sake, not a horny teenager anymore, yet whenever Lana was around, he couldn't seem to control his raging hormones.

What was it about this woman that got to him this way? She was too young for him. Too sweet and fragile. Too *good.*

"Delta!" Le Clair's sharp voice outside the closed door had him shooting to his feet.

It was the perfect excuse he needed to get out of this room, to get away from Lana Kelley before he did something incredibly insane. Like succumb to temptation.

Waiting for his erection to subside, he cast a repentant glance in Lana's direction. She was sitting against the wall, her knees drawn up to her chest and her hands clasped together. Her head lifted to meet his gaze, and the turmoil in her eyes nearly did him in.

"That shouldn't have happened," she whispered.

He let out a breath. "I know." Then he headed out the door, where Le Clair waited for him in the hall.

"How's the princess?" the boss asked casually.

Deacon bit back his irritation. "She's fine. Still a little shaken up, but she'll be all right."

"Good, because we're moving out in the morning."

"What?" he said in surprise.

"It's too risky to keep her here any longer. We don't know who that merc may have contacted, though I suspect he was working alone." Le Clair's gray eyes narrowed. "Either way, I want you out on the perimeter with the others tonight, just in case the soldier told a few friends."

"What makes you think he didn't?"

"Senator Kelley wouldn't have allowed it," was the vague response, and then Le Clair was marching off. "Help Tango load up the truck," he called over his shoulder, already pulling his cell phone from his pocket.

Deacon watched Le Clair go, wariness crawling through him. What the hell was going on here? He wasn't so concerned with the fact that they were leaving; what worried him was that

Le Clair seemed determined to hold on to Lana. This was the time to cut and run. The mercenary's appearance served as an omen of things to come. Soon the authorities would be beating down the door, and once that happened, they were all screwed. It was evident Lana's father wasn't interested in paying the ransom.

So where did that leave Lana?

"Tango," Deacon called as he stepped onto the porch. He headed for the black pickup truck parked in the clearing, where Tango was hauling a few duffel bags into the cab.

The other man turned at the sound of his name, the scar on his cheek puckering as he frowned. "Yeah?"

Deacon picked up a duffel and approached the truck. "Apparently we're moving out," he said.

Tango nodded. "That's the order."

Tossing the bag into the truck, Deacon lowered his voice and added, "What the hell is going on here, man?"

"I don't know." Tango ran a hand through his dark hair. "But it isn't good."

"No kidding."

There was a long pause, followed by an awkward cough from Tango. "Apparently there's another team in Montana."

Deacon raised his head. "Yeah?"

"Yeah. Le Clair let it slip that he's got men watching the senator. Dude's hiding out on some ranch."

"Hiding out? Because he screwed around on his wife?"

Frustration seeped into Tango's harsh features. "I don't know what's going on, bro. But I definitely don't like it."

A dour voice sounded from behind. "They want the father to come forward."

Deacon turned to see Echo approaching. There was a deep crease between the other man's brows. "I overheard Le Clair talking to someone about it."

As if his ears had been burning, Le Clair suddenly appeared on the porch, his cell phone glued to his ear. He cast a suspicious look in the direction of the trio, causing Deacon and Tango to bend down and pick up a metal crate filled to the gills with dynamite. Dynamite, for Chrissake. Why did they need all this crap? This had been supposed to be an easy grab-and-wait.

"What did you hear?" Deacon murmured.

Echo unlatched the cab so that the other two could slide the crate into it. "Apparently old man Kelley is being asked to turn himself in."

"Do you know why? What did he do?" Tango asked.

"No freaking clue. But he's not cooperating, whatever it is." Echo made a frustrated sound under his breath. "Le Clair doesn't know what to do with the girl anymore. Whoever hired us is getting mighty impatient. Le Clair's not too happy, either."

Deacon sneaked a peek at the boss, whose dark eyebrows were bunched together in sheer aggravation. This latest call in a string of phone calls was obviously not going well. Deacon's gut went rigid with trepidation. "I don't like this," he said, echoing Tango's earlier words. "Something's not right with this entire job."

"I hear ya," Tango muttered.

"Ditto," Echo added. "So…what do we do?"

Get Lana the hell out of here.

He swallowed back the words and pasted on an indifferent expression. "We wait," he finally murmured. "Let's get on that plane, see how things play out and figure it out then."

They stored the last of the gear into the truck and latched it up. Deacon was slightly comforted by the fact that his fellow mercenaries shared his concerns, but at the moment, none of them could do a damn thing about it. Whatever was going on in the real world, it wasn't good. Sooner or later, Le Clair would need to fill his men in on whatever it was.

And then Deacon would have to decide if he'd need to save his own skin.

Or protect Lana's.

* * *

Washington, D.C. The irony of their destination didn't escape Lana as the jet began its descent into the city that had caused her family so much turmoil. Le Clair hadn't blindfolded her this time, so she had a clear view of the Washington Monument and the glow of lights from Capitol Hill as the jet headed for the runway below.

She used to visit her dad here when she was a kid. She and her mom lived in California for most of the year, but D.C. was like a second home. Her father's entire life revolved around this darn city, so much so that he'd neglected all of his children, thanks to his high-profile political career.

Why had her captors brought her here? The choice of location troubled her, but also brought a flicker of hope. Maybe this was it. Her dad would give them the money they desired, and an exchange would be made. Maybe she could finally go *home*.

Lana jumped as the wheels connected with the runway, causing the plane to bounce and shudder until it finally came to a complete stop. On the other side of the lavish cabin, Deacon sat next to Tango, and she noticed that both men wore the same serious expression. They didn't look happy about this latest development.

Neither was she.

And she certainly wasn't happy with what had happened last night in the cabin. When she'd nearly *seduced* Deacon.

What had she been thinking?

Nothing at all.

No, she hadn't been thinking last night. Rick Garrison's senseless death had sent her reeling, placed her in a severe state of shock that left her numb and unable to conjure up a single rational thought. Even now, the memory of Garrison's lifeless body caused her pulse to race. Le Clair had murdered that poor man in cold blood, and no matter what Deacon said, she knew she'd be saddled with Garrison's death on her conscience for the rest of her life.

Her hands went cold as the ominous knowledge settled over her like a thick patch of fog. A man had died because of her.

No, because of her *father*. The one person she'd always stood by, given her unconditional love to, no matter how badly he screwed things up with her mother and siblings. Why hadn't her father found a way to rescue her already?

The anger coursing through her came as a total shock. As a child, she'd idolized her dad. As an adult, she'd rationalized his mistakes, tried to see the best in him despite his many flaws.

Maybe she'd been wrong to do that. It was definitely getting harder to ignore everything Hank Kelley had done, especially now. Her father had cheated on her mother. He'd selfishly hurt his wife and Lana's older brothers. And he'd hurt her, too, over the years, no matter how much she tried to deny it. He hadn't even shown up for her college graduation, for Pete's sake. But she'd forgiven him, of course.

She always forgave him, she realized bitterly.

Always gave him the benefit of the doubt, even when her older brothers laughed at her for doing it, teasing her for being an idealistic fool.

But this…could she forgive her father for *this?* She'd been a prisoner for more than a month, and what was her dad doing? Sitting at home drinking his favorite bourbon while he continually refused to pay her ransom?

Why wasn't he *doing* something, damn it?

Lana resisted the urge to cradle her belly. She'd been doing that too often lately, and was fearful that Deacon would start to pick up on the shielding gesture.

So what if he does?

The thought made her hesitate. Maybe it was time to tell Deacon the truth about the baby. She'd been dragging her feet for weeks, but now that the situation seemed to be escalating into something that sent a chill to her bones, she might need to be completely honest with Deacon.

Another SUV greeted them at the airstrip,

and Lana was shoved into the backseat. Still not blindfolded, though, which was a relief. She stared glumly out the tinted window as the familiar scenery whizzed by. The car cruised right by Capitol Hill then veered north, finally coming to a stop on a narrow street near Stanton Park. Low-rise apartment buildings lined each side of the sidewalk. Echo, who was in the driver's seat, drove into an underground parking lot beneath one of the buildings.

The sheer nerve of it amazed her. They were hiding her in plain sight. No isolated cabin this time, but in the heart of the U.S. capital. These men were either very foolish or very smart.

Le Clair hadn't come with them this time. He'd slid into another SUV with Oscar at the airstrip, saying he had a few things to take care of. Lana hoped that meant he was contacting her father again, setting up some kind of exchange, but the nagging twisting of her insides told her she might be hoping for too much.

The four remaining men—Deacon, Echo,

Kilo and Tango—clustered around her as they walked into the elevator in the underground. The car dinged and stopped on the third floor, and then she was being led into a spacious apartment with cream-colored walls, modern furnishings and thick white carpeting.

"Who lives here?" she couldn't help but ask.

None of the men replied. Deacon had her suitcase tucked under one strong arm. He gestured for her to follow him, taking her down the brightly lit hallway toward a bedroom in the back. The master bedroom, judging by the size, and a refreshing change from her previous accommodations. This room was large and airy, with a huge four-poster bed and bright turquoise comforter, a cozy living area with a couch and love seat, and an enormous bathroom off to the left.

"You'll be more comfortable now," he said.

She fixed him with a cool stare. "I'm still a prisoner. A fancy room isn't going to change that."

What looked like remorse flickered in his hazel eyes. "I'm sorry."

She got the feeling he was apologizing for a lot more than simply her current state of captivity.

"How much longer is this going to last, Deacon?" She spoke in a dull voice, not even able to muster up anger anymore.

"I don't know."

"Another week? Another month?"

"I don't know."

The pain on his face was unmistakable. The tug of hope she'd experienced in the car returned, this time wrapping around her entire body like a comforting pair of arms. "You're going to help me," she whispered.

His eyes remained shuttered. "Nothing's been decided yet."

Lana moved toward him. Before she could stop herself, she had both her hands on his chin. She forced him to meet her gaze. "No, you've already decided. You don't like what's happening here any more than I do."

"No," he agreed quietly.

Her hands dropped to her sides in determined fists. "Then let's get out of here. I promise you, I won't let them arrest you. I'll do everything I can to make sure the authorities know you're not to blame for any of this."

His eyebrows shot up to his forehead. Her words surprised her as much as they did him. She hadn't planned on saying that, but once it was out, she realized she didn't want to take it back. She *didn't* want to see Deacon punished for this. Maybe it made her the idiot of the century, but she was still clinging to the notion that he was a good man.

"You'd do that for me?" He sounded gruff. And slightly ashamed. As if he couldn't possibly fathom how she could make him an offer like that.

"This wasn't your idea." She studied his face. "You got caught up in something that spun out of control. And you've been doing everything in your power to keep me safe. I'll make sure the cops know that."

"Why?"

Because you're the father of my baby.

The confession almost popped out, but jammed in her throat at the last second. Not yet. She couldn't tell him yet. He was beginning to give in, to recognize that they truly needed to get themselves out of this mess. If she told him about the baby now, he might shut down again and dismiss her plan.

She couldn't risk that.

"Because I have to believe you're a good person," was what she said instead.

He shifted in discomfort, his broad shoulders sagging. "Why are you so determined to believe that? I'm not the man you think I am. I'm not—"

"Delta." Tango's sharp voice came from the doorway.

Both Lana and Deacon turned to look at him.

She noticed that Tango's scar was stretched tight over his cheek, his expression taut with suspicion. Oh, crap. Had he overheard what they'd been talking about?

She studied his face, but he gave no sign that he'd heard anything of importance. "We need you to help secure the apartment," he muttered to Deacon.

With a nod, Deacon headed for the door. "I'll bring you some lunch shortly," he said to her without turning around.

She watched the two men go, listened to the sound of yet another lock sliding into place.

Lana released a troubled breath. Okay. She was locked up again. But this time, the hope swimming through her remained strong. Steady. Deacon was slowly coming over to her side. He'd heard everything she'd said right now. He'd even seemed to be considering it.

All she could do now was pray that she'd gotten through to him.

* * *

A week passed before Hank called with another update. The last Sarah had heard, her husband had hired a mercenary to retrieve their daughter. Since then, she'd been going out of her mind with panic, conjuring up so many worst-case scenarios she couldn't even remember what living without fear had been like.

When the phone finally rang, she was in Vivienne's kitchen, staring at a glass emptied of red wine. Viv had flown back to California to be with her children—she had two young teenagers who needed constant attention—but she'd made it clear that Sarah could stay in the Vineyard beach house for as long as she needed.

Sarah had been tempted to return to California, too, but the thought of being alone in the Beverly Hills mansion she'd shared with her husband sent sorrow spinning through her. She couldn't face the past yet, not when her future with Hank was still up in the air. Not when her daughter had been a prisoner for more than a month.

"It's not good," were Hank Kelley's first words.

Terror seized her heart. "Is she alive?"

"As far as I know." He let out a heavy breath. "But the man I sent to rescue her isn't."

"What?"

"They killed him, Sarah. He was supposed to be one of the best, and these sons of bitches managed to kill him." Agony rang from his voice. "Cole found the body. Those bastards dropped him off right on the doorstep, a bullet between his eyes."

Sarah almost fainted. The phone fell from her hands, clattering against the white marble counter. She dropped her head in her hands and sucked in desperate breaths, fighting the wave of lightheadedness ripping through her.

"Sarah. Sarah! *Sarah!*"

Hank's voice thudded from the phone. She finally picked up the cell. "I'm here," she croaked. "I'm... Oh, lord, Hank, who *are* these people?"

He didn't reply.

"You need to call the FBI," she burst out. "And I'm calling Jim."

"Not yet," Hank blurted. "I promise you, darling, I'm taking care of it. I'm going to demand proof of life the next time they call, which should be any second now. They're going to want to brag about their latest surprise."

"Proof of life?" she echoed warily.

"I don't want to involve anyone else until I know without a doubt that Lana is still alive. For all we know, they're just playing with us."

Another wave of dizziness. The mere thought of Lana being gone made her belly tighten with uncontrollable grief. "Jim might be able to help."

"No. I'm not dragging another one of our children into this mess. I wouldn't be able to live myself if something happened to that boy. Losing Lana is already bad enough."

"We haven't lost her," she choked out. "Don't say things like that."

A heavy breath filled the line. "I know. I'm sorry." He paused. "Just sit tight, darling. I'm going to make some calls, and I hope the men who have our daughter will contact me soon. Trust me. I'll be in touch, Sarah."

They disconnected, and Sarah's head dropped right back between her hands. Tears filled her eyes. *Trust me.*

How could he even ask her that, after everything he'd done to their family? But what choice did she have?

She wanted her daughter back, and Hank was right. If they involved anyone else right now, the kidnappers could panic and kill Lana. If they hadn't done so already.

She gathered up every iota of strength in her body, slowly lifting her head. It was becoming glaringly obvious that if she wanted her daughter home safe and sound, she really did need to do the impossible.

Trust her husband again.

Chapter 10

Lana feared her words must have fallen on deaf ears. Another miserable week had gone by, and she was still in D.C., in this lavish bedroom that only served as a reminder that whoever was calling the shots must have a truckload of cash at their disposal. This was no amateur operation. Le Clair's bosses were no doubt loaded, which meant they had to be extremely important people.

Her father had plenty of political enemies, but Lana couldn't even imagine the kind of power needed to undertake this scheme. It was definitely an expensive mission. Deacon and the others must be earning a huge amount of money for them to involve themselves in such a risky and time-consuming assignment, and Le Clair was probably pulling in a hefty amount of dough, too. Not to mention the state-of-the-art equipment, the weapons, the private jet, this fancy apartment. Whoever these men were, they had a lot of money, and a lot of time.

Unfortunately, time wasn't on her side here. The pregnancy would start to show soon, yet she still couldn't bring herself to tell Deacon about the baby. Each time she tried, the words got stuck in her throat like a wad of bubble gum, and she ended up swallowing them down where they congealed into a painful lump in her belly.

What would happen when she started showing? Sure, it might be another month from now—two even—but what if she was still a hostage at that point? Deacon hadn't commented on the fullness of her breasts when he'd had his hands on them back at the cabin, but there was no way she'd be able to hide a baby bump from him. Or the others.

She grew sick at the thought, as she pondered Le Clair's volatile reaction if he learned his hostage was pregnant.

When Deacon came into the room, she was still thinking about her dilemma, but any urge to blurt out the truth was squashed when Le Clair appeared at Deacon's heels. Echo came in, too, and Lana's chest tightened when she saw the sleek camcorder in his hands.

"What's going on?" she asked uneasily.

"Your daddy thinks we killed you," Le Clair explained, an irritated frown curling his lips. "We're here to ease his mind."

As usual, Le Clair's accented voice was cheerful. She imagined him using that same tone while cold-bloodedly killing someone.

Wait, she didn't even have to imagine. She'd witnessed it firsthand already.

Echo moved over to the living area, as Le Clair gestured for her to sit down on the love seat. She noticed he made sure to keep her away from the window, in order to ensure that their location wasn't revealed.

With great weariness, Lana sat down. Not because she'd been ordered to, but because frankly, she was exhausted. The constant worry and panic battling in her belly were starting to wear her down. She barely even reacted when Le Clair thrust a piece of paper in her hands.

"What's this?" she asked woodenly.

"Your script." He bared his teeth in a cheerless smile. "Please don't deviate. I'd really like to get this in one take."

She glanced down at the words scrawled on the paper. "What does this mean?"

"Don't you worry about that, princess. Just say what's written."

Echo stepped forward, holding the camera. A red light blinked under the lens, indicating he was recording. Le Clair came up beside his goon, signaling with an impatient gesture for her to begin.

"As you can see, I'm alive," she recited. "And I will stay that way as long as you cooperate."

She hesitated, shooting a desperate look at Deacon, who gave an imperceptible nod. He wanted her to keep going. But that one sentence on the page—it glared up at her like an accusation. And her insides were tied in fearful knots. If she said these words, something bad would happen to her father. She felt it deep in her bones. And as angry as she was with him right now, as hard as it was to accept that her father was the reason she was here, she refused to let anything happen to Hank. She would die before she saw him hurt.

Le Clair waved his hand angrily, his silver eyes blazing with annoyance.

Lana took a breath. "So please, Dad," she said in a wobbly voice. "Come forward and turn yourself in. It's the only way to—"

Abruptly, she halted. A wave of defiance swept through her, carrying away the numbness that had plagued her body all week and replacing it with white-hot anger. Enough. She wasn't playing these damned games anymore. At this point, if these men wanted to kill her, *let* them.

She was no longer interested in meek obedience.

"Don't do what they say, Daddy!" she blurted out, fixing a steely gaze into the camera lens. "They're going to kill me regardless—"

Pain collided with her cheek as Le Clair's fist came crashing down on her jaw, jerking her head back with incredible force. Then he moved back, completely unruffled, while her jaw throbbed relentlessly, flushing and swelling from the assault. He'd kept his back to the camera, keeping his identity hidden, and he didn't say a word as he stepped out of the frame and gestured for Echo to stop filming.

"We doing it again?" Echo said, sounding resigned.

Le Clair paused, a thoughtful expression crossing his angular face. "No," he finally decided. "Despite the deviation, I think this will have the precise impact I'm looking for."

With that, Le Clair stalked out of the room, Echo on his tail. Deacon remained, and he turned to look at her with both concern and dismay.

"Why do you keep doing this?" he asked hoarsely. "You need to stop goading that bastard."

He walked over to the sofa, hesitated for a beat, then knelt down in front of her. One large warm hand touched her jaw, a tender caress to gauge the injury. "Are you okay?" His hazel eyes searched her face.

She opened and closed her mouth a few times, testing the pain. "I'm fine. It doesn't even hurt anymore."

"Good."

She expected him to get up, but he stayed on his knees. Even in that position, he was so big. So masculine. Despite herself, Lana found her pulse speeding up. His now-familiar scent of spice and soap surrounded her, teasing her senses, and his strong, corded neck bobbed as he visibly swallowed. She felt the urge to wrap her arms around him. To bury her face against that muscular chest, just so she could feel safe for a few fleeting seconds.

Which was a total joke. She *wasn't* safe. As long as she was being held prisoner, she'd never be safe.

"This..." Deacon cleared his throat, but when he spoke, his voice still came out rusty. "This is killing me, Lana."

Surprise flitted through her. Her throat tightened, making it difficult to speak, so she just stared into his serious brown-green eyes like a mute.

"I can't stand seeing him do that to you." The confession seemed painful for him, as if he wasn't comfortable revealing weakness. Wasn't happy letting go of his iron control. "When he hit you just now... Jesus, Lana, I wanted to strangle him."

"You would've gotten us both killed," she said softly.

"I know." He covered her knees with his hands, holding on tight, but she got the feeling he didn't even realize what he was doing. Despair blazed in his eyes, along with an emotion she couldn't put her finger on. "You're right. We need to do something."

Hope surrounded her heart. "Are you serious?"

He nodded. "Whatever's happening here, it isn't good. I don't know what Le Clair's bosses want from your dad, but I don't think it's money. And I don't think Le Clair ever planned on letting you get out of this alive."

Her breath hitched in fear. "He's going to kill me."

Deacon's shoulders fell. "I think so."

Without thinking about what she was doing, she covered his hands with her own. "Then we have to get out of here before that happens." She squeezed his knuckles and met his tortured gaze. "Will you help me?"

After a long moment of silence, he nodded again.

Another burst of hope exploded in her chest. "Tonight?"

A swift shake of the head. "No. I need to think about the best way to do this."

"Okay," she conceded.

"And until I come up with a plan, you have to promise me you won't antagonize Le Clair anymore. Keep following his orders, don't cause trouble. I don't want him suspecting that something might be up."

She gave another, "Okay."

They sat there for a few seconds, Deacon on his knees, Lana on the couch. Their hands were still touching, and warmth sizzled between them.

"Thank you," she finally whispered.

Hank called just as Sarah was stepping out of the shower, her hair dripping water onto her bare shoulders. She dashed for the cell phone she'd left on the dresser.

"Did you get proof of life?" She nearly shouted the question, not bothering with hello.

"Yes."

She almost keeled over with relief. "Then she's alive."

"Yes. We got a video." Hank hesitated. "He hit her."

"What?"

"From what we gathered, they were making her read from a script, and she didn't cooperate."

Sarah felt lightheaded. Oh, Lana. Her baby girl had always been incredibly calm under pressure, but every now and then that headstrong streak of hers reared its ugly head.

"The man in charge didn't like what she said, so he punched her in the jaw." Hank sounded absolutely destroyed. "God, Sarah, it was so difficult to watch."

She could imagine. The mere thought of some

goon striking her baby girl was enough to send a primal wave of fury through her. Like a mama lioness, she wanted to protect her cub, suddenly wishing the bastard were right here so she could claw his eyes out.

"But she's alive," she said, forcing herself to look on the bright side.

"Yes."

"So what now?"

There was a beat of silence. "Now I give myself up."

Shock jolted into her. "What the hell are you talking about? Now we call the FBI!"

"I already did."

"Thank God," she said in relief.

"But their presence won't change a damn thing. I'm the only one who can save our girl, Sarah."

Her stomach tightened with fear. God, he'd gone absolutely insane. "You can't do this, Hank. You'll get Lana *and* yourself killed if you try to negotiate with these people on your own. We need to be smart here."

"I am being smart. I've caused enough damage, Sarah." Determination hardened his tone. "I got us into this mess, and I'm sure as hell going to get us out of it. I'll be in touch, darling."

"Hank—"

The telltale click in her ear told her he'd hung up. Sarah sank onto the edge of the bed, feeling as if she'd just had the wind knocked out of her. That stubborn *jerk!* Why couldn't he make an *intelligent* decision for once in his sorry life?

Her hands shook wildly as she brought up the contact list on her cell phone. Enough was enough. She wasn't letting Hank Kelley put his life, or their daughter's, in danger. Not for a second longer.

A chipper voice answered the phone as she was connected with the military base. "Put me through to Colonel Keaton," she demanded, her unsteady voice betraying her lack of confidence.

"Who may I tell him is calling?"

"Sarah Mistler Kelley."

There was a tiny beat as the switchboard operator must have recognized the name, and then, "Right away, ma'am."

Several seconds later, Keaton came on the line, barking out his name and rank.

Beating straight to the punch, Sarah introduced herself then said, "Colonel, I need you to get an urgent message to Captain Jim Kelley."

As the days ticked by on Deacon's mental calendar, he wondered if he'd ever be able to keep his promise to Lana. He hadn't changed his mind, though. Not by a long shot. After that video-camera scene with Le Clair, along with the conversation he'd had with Echo and Tango, he was more convinced than ever that he needed to get Lana out of here. The only glitch was, Le Clair wasn't going anywhere.

Back at the cabin, the boss had hopped the jet several times, leaving his men in charge. Deacon suspected he was meeting with whoever had hired him, and then, of course, there was the trip to Montana, where, according to Echo, the mercenary's body had been dumped. With Le Clair breathing down their necks, Deacon was stuck. He'd already decided that he needed Le Clair gone in order to liberate Lana. He'd formulated a plan, gone over the details a hundred times, but he couldn't execute it until Le Clair took one of his day trips. Which for the moment, didn't seem to be happening.

There was a chill in the air as Deacon walked along the quiet sidewalk toward the apartment building. The men had been assigned to monitor the street in teams, to ensure the location remained secure. Tango walked a few yards away, on the other side of the road, looking very nondescript with his head buried in a newspaper. But like Deacon, Tango was on guard, watching the neighborhood for any sign of police presence. There was none, and Deacon wasn't sure if he was relieved or annoyed as he headed into the lobby.

He almost wished the cops would come pounding on the door. He'd taken on risky jobs in the past, a couple of kidnappings involving shady CEOs, the killing of a South American rebel leader who'd been selling little girls in the sex trade. Not once had he felt an ounce of guilt during those missions. He'd felt no pity for the men he'd helped abduct, no remorse when he put a bullet in that rebel's head.

But this job was different. Lana Kelley was a good person, right down to her core, and she didn't deserve a single minute of what had happened to her. And Le Clair was just sitting around, constantly whispering into his cell phone, as if the big guns in charge didn't know themselves what the next step would be.

Whatever it was, Deacon knew it wouldn't bode well for Lana, and he was determined to do something to change that.

He might be a cold bastard, but he refused to let this woman die. He'd done a lot of things in his life, most of them less than pleasant, but the killing of an innocent? That was something he'd never been—and never wanted to be—a part of.

It didn't help that Lana Kelley had completely gotten under his skin. Each moment he spent with her only heightened his respect for the fresh-faced beauty. He suspected she might be stronger than he'd ever be. Not to mention smart and kind and unbelievably forgiving. She should loathe him for his part in this, but she didn't. She should shy away from his touch, but she didn't.

He didn't deserve that kind of trust, but maybe if he saved her…maybe if he made sure she survived this, he might find some sort of redemption.

When he entered the apartment, he heard activity in the back bedroom. Immediately his guard shot up. If Le Clair was doing anything to hurt Lana, he knew without a doubt that he would kill the bastard.

What he found, however, was another impromptu performance, this one involving a digital camera held by Echo and a copy of the day's newspaper clutched by Lana. The flash went off a couple of times, as a stoic-faced Echo snapped Lana's picture.

Deacon could imagine how the Kelley family would react when they received the photo. Lana's beautiful face was as pale as the white wall behind her. Smudges of exhaustion marred her ashen face, and her lips were set in a tired line. As she'd promised him, she sat there obediently, not once acting on the flicker of anger he saw lurking in the shadows of her eyes.

He smothered a wild groan. Why was this still going on? The video, the pictures, the pointless phone calls—he got the feeling this was all being done for theatrics, and when Le Clair clapped his hands to signal the shoot was over and offered Lana a gracious smile, Deacon's suspicions were only confirmed.

This was a game. A sick, twisted, waste-of-time game.

The boss spotted Deacon in the doorway and headed his way. They stepped out into the hall, followed by Echo, who was studying the photos he'd just captured. He handed the camera to Le Clair, who glanced at the pictures and nodded in approval.

"Good job," Le Clair said. He closed the door to Lana's room, then turned to face them. "I'm heading out. Man the fort while I'm gone."

Deacon's chest flooded with satisfaction. Yes. *Finally.*

"How long will you be gone?" he asked tentatively.

"A day. Two at the most. The exchange is being set up."

Deacon's satisfaction faded into concern. Crap. That didn't sound good. Maybe the game was reaching its end point.

"Exchange?" he echoed.

Le Clair looked smug. "The good senator has agreed to sacrifice himself for his little girl."

What the hell did that mean? Although Deacon had suspected it for a long time, it now became painfully obvious that money had never been a factor in this equation. Whatever Le Clair's bosses wanted from Hank Kelley, it wasn't his cash.

The fact that Le Clair spoke of an "exchange" did nothing to convince Deacon that the man planned on letting Lana go. He sensed this was one big trap, and that in the end, both father and daughter would wind up dead.

Good thing he was getting her out of here. Tonight.

After Le Clair left, Deacon prepared lunch for Lana, then walked into the bedroom he'd been sharing with Echo and quietly got his gear together. He slid the packed duffel under the bed with the toe of his black boot, then spent the rest of the day out in the November cold, watching the apartment as ordered. By five-thirty, the sun dipped toward the horizon, darkening the sky to a burnt orange.

It was time.

He entered the building just as Echo and Tango exited to take over the perimeter. With Kilo up on the roof with his rifle, Deacon had only one fellow kidnapper to contend with: Oscar.

As they rode the elevator up to the third floor, Deacon fought a wave of unease. He would've preferred someone other than Oscar in the apartment. Out of all the men, Oscar was definitely the biggest wild card. Somber-faced, distant and disgustingly in awe of Le Clair. But the quick ease with which he responded to Le Clair's commands could prove useful here.

"Crap, I forgot to grab a thermometer," Deacon said as he and Oscar entered the living room.

Oscar glanced over blankly. "What?"

"Le Clair asked me to pick one up from the

drugstore over on the next block." Deacon made a big show of looking frazzled—running a hand through his hair, shifting impatiently. "The princess complained she's coming down with the flu. He wants to make sure this isn't a ploy on her part." Now he looked at the watch strapped to his wrist, frowning. "Do you know how to cook?"

The vacant look only deepened. "Huh?"

Deacon had grown used to the monosyllabic grunts that seemed to be the whole of Oscar's vocabulary, other than "yes, sir," of course.

"We need to bring her dinner." Deacon tilted his head. "I'm in charge of the cooking, but you'll need to do it if I'm going to run to the drugstore."

Oscar's dark eyes flitted in the direction of the kitchen, and he noticeably cringed. Deacon hid a grin. He had been banking on the man's lack of culinary prowess.

"Unless you'd rather do the drugstore run," he offered graciously.

The other man brightened. "Yeah. Yeah, I'll d'that. Thermometer, y'said?"

That was another one of Oscar's speech glitches, forming contractions of words that had no business being joined. Deacon resisted the urge to roll his eyes, instead pasting on a grateful expression. "That would be great. And pick up some cold and flu medication, something over the counter, just in case the girl really is coming down with something."

He got a grunt in response. Oscar was already heading to the door. "B'back soon."

"Thanks, buddy," Deacon called after Oscar's retreating back.

Once the door of the apartment closed, Deacon exploded into action. He raced into the bedroom and grabbed his duffel bag, slung it over his shoulder, then marched into Lana's room.

She was sound asleep on the bed, lying on her back. Deacon hesitated for a moment, his gaze sweeping over the sleeping beauty, admiring her smooth aristocratic features, the long blond tresses fanned across the white pillow beneath her head. He forced himself to snap out of it— he could admire her *after* they got away—and hurried to the bed, where he sat down on the edge and gently clapped a hand over her mouth.

Those big blue eyes snapped open, and her muffled scream lasted all of a second, dying abruptly the moment she saw his face. His heart squeezed when he glimpsed the burst of hope in her eyes.

God, he hoped he wasn't sentencing them both to death here.

"Now?" she whispered.

He nodded grimly. "Now."

Chapter 11

Adrenaline pumped through Lana's blood as she followed Deacon out of the bedroom and into the luxurious living area. She half expected armed men to pop out of the corridor and spit bullets at them, but to her shock, the apartment was empty.

"Where is everybody?"

"Outside." That grim look on Deacon's face intensified. "Which is when we need to start worrying."

They moved out of the apartment with lightning speed. Deacon had a duffel over his shoulder and a gun in his right hand, which he kept trained straight ahead as they sprinted to the stairwell. It was only three flights down, but by the time they made it to the bottom landing, Lana was panting like a thirsty dog. Her heart thudded in her chest, each frantic beat bringing a jolt of fear and jubilation.

He was saving her! And risking Le Clair's wrath in order to do it. She couldn't help but shoot him a look loaded with relief, but his profile was hard with concentration.

Shoving his gun in the waistband of his pants, he covered it with the hem of his sweater and said, "There's a car parked at the end of the street. When we get outside, you keep your head down and walk beside me. If I say run, you need to run. Do you understand?"

"Yes."

"Good. Let's go."

The heavy stairwell door creaked as Deacon pushed it open. They came into a bright lobby with two plush white sofas in front of the elevator bank. Empty. Lana could practically taste

Deacon's relief. It was coating her mouth, too. As she'd promised, she kept her head down, sticking close to Deacon as they walked through the glass double doors at the building's entrance and stepped outside.

The early winter breeze snaked underneath her hair, cooling her neck. Deacon hadn't given her time to grab a coat before appearing in the bedroom and whisking her out of the apartment. Her breath left visible white clouds in the air as they made their way onto the sidewalk. They kept to a brisk pace, almost a jog, and Lana was certain they'd made it unnoticed.

Until the No Parking sign right above her head burst apart from the force of a bullet. Metal shards went flying, one nearly clipping her ear.

"Run," Deacon barked out, yanking on her arm.

Her heart nearly ripped out of her chest. Gunshots! The others were shooting at them! The cement of the sidewalk exploded beneath her feet, as the shooter decided to go for a leg shot to stop them. Lana's head spun from Deacon's random zigzag sprint. He was making sure the shooter couldn't find a target, but the zigzagging made her dizzy.

"Delta! Don't move!"

A voice shouted at them, and Lana couldn't help herself—she glanced over her shoulder. An infuriated Oscar was running after them, his gun raised. Deacon tugged on her arm, forcing her to keep moving. Panic torpedoed into her when another angry voice joined Oscar's. Echo or Tango, and now more footsteps thudding from behind.

"We're not going to make it," she cried.

"We'll make it." Deacon's voice came out in sharp pants.

They ran. Lana's heart slapped against her ribs. She sucked in gulps of cold air, her boots clacking a staccato rhythm against the sidewalk. A car finally came into view, a black sedan, parked at the curb. It was the only vehicle on the street. Twenty feet. Ten feet.

They were almost there. They were going to make it!

Pain exploded in Lana's left arm.

She stumbled forward with a cry, as waves of agony pulsed through her body. Stars flashed in front of her eyes, but Deacon forced her to keep running. Five feet. Three. Two. Gravity eluded her as she was suddenly thrown into the passenger seat of the sedan, while moisture seeped into the sleeve of her pale blue sweater.

She stared down at her arm. A crimson stain had bloomed in the material of the sweater. She'd been shot. Shot. And she was bleeding heavily, her entire arm wet and sticky with blood.

"The baby," she mumbled to herself.

A car door slammed and she blinked in terror, only to realize it was Deacon sliding into the driver's seat. He bent under the dashboard of the car, flicked a few wires together, and the car roared to life.

"Get your head down!" Deacon shouted at her.

She ducked, burying her face in her lap just as the back windshield of the car shattered. Shards of glass flew into the front seat, lodging in Lana's hair and nicking her ear. She sucked in oxygen. Felt her head spinning as the pain in her arm throbbed. As the blood coated the armrest between her and Deacon.

"Oh, God," she whispered. What if she lost too much blood? What if she lost the baby?

The car lurched forward as Deacon slammed a foot down on the gas pedal. Rubber squealed, another bullet rocked the car, then another, dinging off their bumper like a ball colliding into the walls of an arcade pinball machine.

"Where are you hit?" came Deacon's frantic voice.

And then his hand was on her arm, the contact bringing a sharp wave of nausea to her belly. Something ripped. The sleeve of her sweater, she realized. Deacon made a sound between a growl and curse as he ran his bare hand over her blood-soaked skin.

"Lana. Lana! Quit hitting me and let me examine the wound."

Hitting him? She hadn't even realized she was doing it. Taking in short, panicked bursts of air, she went motionless, biting her lip through the pain as Deacon appraised her wound. Somehow he managed to keep his eyes on the road ahead and at the same time wrap the sleeve he'd torn off around her arm in a tight tourniquet.

"It's a flesh wound," he assured her. "You're going to be fine, sweetheart. It looks bad, I know, but it was just a graze."

His words barely even registered. She was too busy staring at the blood. So much blood. Sticking to the armrest. Spattered on the beige leather seat.

"The baby," she whispered, breathing through the white-hot pulses of pain. "Oh, Deacon, the *baby.*"

She felt more than saw his head swivel at her in complete shock. "What did you say?"

"I'm pregnant." Teardrops slid down her cheeks, falling onto the seat and mingling with the blood. "I…" Her heart twisted in her chest. "I *can't* lose our baby. I can't." She clung to her injured arm, her tears soaking the tourniquet. "Promise me I won't lose it. *Promise* me."

Deacon felt as though he'd been punched in the gut, followed by the swing of a baseball bat to his head. His stomach roiled, his head spun and the Vatican should have been contacted, because it was a sheer miracle that he managed to drive away in the stolen car without smashing into the nearest tree.

Pregnant.

Pregnant?

Was this a joke? How could she be pregnant?

Okay, well, he knew *how*. But why? They'd used protection.

If you called an ancient condom that had been stuffed in his wallet years ago protection.

Deacon fought a wild curse. Why hadn't he checked the damn expiration date on the latex?

How could Lana be *pregnant?*

He stared dumbfounded at her for several long seconds, then jerked out of it when a honk wailed in the air. He straightened the wheel before a head-on collision could destroy his and Lana's chances for escape.

Focus.

Deacon focused. He shoved Lana's shocking confession from his mind and concentrated on the road ahead, maneuvering through the streets of D.C. There'd be plenty of time to freak out later. Right now they just needed to get the hell out of Dodge.

"You okay?" he asked roughly as he zipped onto the on ramp of the highway.

She nodded, but he noticed she was shaking hysterically as she continued to put pressure on her wound. Her blond hair was stuck to her cheeks, and tears continued to flow from her eyes. She was scared. Every pore in her body radiated fear. Despite himself, he glanced down at her stomach, flat beneath her blue sweater.

Pregnant. Jesus Christ.

Shaking the thought right out of his head, he drove until they reached the next exit, constantly flicking his gaze to the rearview mirror to make sure they weren't being tailed. A higher power had been smiling down on them earlier. Lana might have been hit, but the others hadn't had time to find a vehicle and finish the job. The SUV was parked in the underground, which meant Deacon had a head start on his former partners in crime.

He sped down the exit ramp, moving his head left and right until he spotted a small strip mall at the corner of the intersection. Steering toward it, he drove into the lot, parked the car and reached for Lana.

She blinked in surprise. "Why did we stop?"

she whispered. It was the first sentence she'd uttered since dropping her bomb of a confession.

"We need to switch cars." He unbuckled her seat belt, then hopped out of the car, rounded it and helped Lana out of the passenger seat.

She sagged into him, her blond hair tickling his chin as she rested her head against his shoulder. He quickly scouted the lot and led her to a small Toyota near the back. An older model, didn't even have an alarm. Deacon hotwired the thing in less than two minutes flat and then they were on the road again, heading out of the city.

They wound up at a small, weathered-looking motel beyond the Virginia border. Deacon would've kept driving for several more hours if not for Lana's injury. He needed to clean up that bullet wound and take a closer look at the damage. At least she hadn't lost consciousness. She'd been awake the entire ride, her gaze glued out the window. She hadn't said a single word.

Shock? Or had her confession troubled her as much as it did him?

Deacon kept his head low as he ducked into the tiny office and paid for a room. The guy at the desk, a skinny teenager with a shaved head and a nose ring, didn't even react when Deacon signed a fake name on the registry. Deacon paid cash, accepted a big red key with the number 8 on it and got back in the car, steering it toward the far end of the lot.

He parked in front of room eight and turned to Lana. "We're here," he said gruffly.

She just nodded and reached to unbuckle her seat belt. The two of them got out of the sedan and Deacon unlocked the room door. He went in first, drawing his weapon out of habit to clear the room before Lana stepped inside. When he flicked on the light, she blinked like a disoriented Alzheimer's patient. Her blue eyes took in the ugly orange bedspread, splintered wooden table and frayed brown carpet. She seemed completely unaffected by the shabbiness.

"Sit down on the bed," he said, already bending down to unzip his duffel.

He took out the first-aid kit and sat next to Lana. She winced as he gently removed the scrap of material from her arm. Dried blood was caked onto her fair skin, bringing a rush of fury to his gut. Those bastards had shot Lana. As the rage-inducing revelation entered his brain, Deacon curled his fists and drew in a calming breath. He wanted to strike something, but he couldn't. Not now, not until he made sure Lana was all right.

After that, though...well, he knew that he'd hunt down the man who'd pulled the trigger, even if he spent the rest of his life hunting. Echo, Tango, Oscar—he didn't care who it was. The man was *dead*.

Lana made a hissing sound as he placed a piece of gauze soaked with rubbing alcohol directly on her skin. "Sorry," he said hoarsely. "I'll be quick."

He skillfully cleaned the wound, not a stranger to the task. He'd had to self-treat dozens of times over the years. Once her arm had been cleaned, he examined the injury, pleased to find that the bullet hadn't even gone through. It had simply grazed her, leaving a red streak resembling a burn on her skin.

"Almost done," he murmured.

Lana didn't say a word as he gently placed a square bandage on her arm and taped it down. When he'd finished, he picked up the blood-stained gauzes, threw them into the garbage can in the closet-size bathroom and returned to the room to find Lana rubbing her stomach with shaky hands.

Her blue eyes met his. "I guess I should have told you sooner." Her voice was soft, wry almost.

"Probably," he agreed.

He moved back to the bed and sat down. Their knees touched. An involuntary wave of heat swelled inside him. He forced the rising arousal down. This wasn't the time. The adrenaline high from the past couple of hours had succeeded in making him hard, a common affliction among soldiers apparently, but right now, he needed that arousal to go away.

"It happened the night at the Louvre." And then, as if he'd questioned her, she added, "You're the father."

"I figured as much."

A short silence fell.

"Are you…" He cleared his throat, searching for something to say. The right thing. Anything. "You haven't been sick."

"No. Maybe it's too early." She shrugged. "Or maybe I'll be one of the lucky ones who don't suffer from morning sickness."

"Can you…can you feel it move?" The crack in his voice stunned him.

She shook her head. "Definitely too early for that."

Another heavy silence. Deacon's brain couldn't keep up with the conversation, and they were barely talking. A baby. Those were the only two words he could grasp at the moment. Lana was pregnant with his baby.

"A baby," he mumbled under his breath.

For the first time since she'd gotten hurt, a tiny smile lifted the corner of Lana's mouth. "I know, right? I've known for two months, and I'm still surprised by it."

Surprised? Try scared out of his wits.

What on earth would he do with a baby? He wasn't equipped for this. Send him into the jungle with a machine gun, and he'd level anything in front of him. Put a baby in his arms?

His pulse sped up, panic gathering in his stomach. He'd lived up to his promise—he'd rescued her from Le Clair. Did he owe her more than that? Did she expect him to be a father to this kid? Did he *want* to be?

A million questions flew through his mind. The only answer he had, though, the only solid, concrete thing he knew, was that he owed her.

He owed Lana Kelley so much more than he could ever repay. He hadn't signed up for this. He'd been promised a quick job, a way to score a huge chunk of change. Instead, Lana had been a hostage for months, at the mercy of Le Clair and his ruthless fists, forced to pose for videos and photos in order to scare her family.

And the entire time, she'd been pregnant. So yeah, he owed her big-time.

But he couldn't be a father to this baby. He had no love to give to a child, to give to *anybody.* His capacity for love had died right along with his parents years ago. Yet he knew Lana wouldn't be able to understand why he had no place in a kid's life. In *her* life. What if he snapped one day, the way his father had? Genetics were a very powerful thing, and his dad's abusive DNA bubbled like acid in his blood.

As a kid, he'd always been too intense, felt things too deeply, wanted things too much. His father had been like that, too, and after his parents died, Deacon realized just how dangerous that intensity could be. How easily a person could snap.

So he'd banished emotions from his life. Decided the only way to control them was by not feeling them. How could he risk feeling anything for Lana or this baby? What if that darkness inside him, the same darkness that had destroyed his father, slithered out and hurt them? No, he couldn't take that chance. He'd already hurt Lana enough.

The baby would be better off without him. With Lana for a mother, the child would have everything it wanted and needed. Money, security, love, kindness. Deacon knew without a doubt that Lana would be strong for this baby, as strong as she'd been throughout this entire ordeal. An ordeal he was partly responsible for.

Guilt seared into him, nearly burning him alive.

"You...you're the strongest woman I've ever met," he choked out.

Lana stared at him in shock. She must have heard the raw note slicing his voice. *He'd* heard it. And he was just as shocked.

"What?"

Unable to stop himself, he touched her chin,

tracing her delicate jaw with one calloused finger. "You survived this, all of this, with no help from me." Remorse hung from his words. "This entire time, you were strong, for yourself, for this baby. Jesus, Lana, I'm...I'm *in awe* of you."

Rather than shying away, she leaned into his touch, letting him caress her cheek. "You did help," she said quietly. "You got me out."

His chest ached with shame. "I got you *into* this in the first place." The ache was suddenly replaced with a jolt of determination. "But I'm going to fix it. We're not in the clear yet, but I promise you, I'm going to take you back to your family. One of the guys mentioned your father is in Montana, so the first thing we need to do is—"

The feel of her hand on his thigh cut him short. When he met her eyes, he knew exactly what was on her mind.

"Lana..." He trailed off, nearly jumping as she dragged her hand closer to his groin. "Stop."

"No." Her hand stilled. "I know there's a thousand things we need to do, and I *know* that this isn't one of them." Her face collapsed abruptly, a look of torment and dismay entering her eyes. "But damn it, Deacon, I don't want to stop."

She slid closer, pressing her lips on the stubble coating his cheek. "I don't want to think about anything right now. Not our next move, not the fact that we're probably being hunted down as we speak." Her voice shook. "I'm scared and confused, and my arm hurts, and I'm not thinking clearly, and right now, I just want you to kiss me."

His breath hitched.

"Can you do that?" she asked, looking up at him with imploring blue eyes. "Can you please just kiss me?"

Chapter 12

Words kept streaming out of Lana's mouth. Words she knew she shouldn't say, questions she knew she shouldn't ask, but as she sat there next to Deacon, with his big warm body pressed beside hers, she had no strength left. The attraction she'd felt toward this man, however inappropriate it might be, was something she couldn't battle any longer.

This entire night had been too much to handle: fleeing the city, the fear spinning through her at the thought of losing her baby, telling Deacon the truth. She didn't even have the energy to think about any of it right now. She was tired and sore, and so incredibly frightened her hands refused to stop shaking.

"I don't want to think right now," she whispered into his rough, stubble-covered jaw. "I just want to forget about reality."

Deacon didn't respond, but she saw his throat bob as he swallowed.

"That night at the hotel," she continued, a desperate twinge to her voice. "It was like a fantasy, a dream. You made me feel something I've never felt before with a man."

"What did you feel?" His voice came out husky.

"Happy." She moved closer, resting her trembling hands on his broad shoulders. "I was happy that night. It was…it was exciting and passionate. I couldn't even remember my own name afterward."

He swallowed again, then said, "Me, too."

"So let's deal with this mess in the morning." She twined her arms around his neck. "Right now, let's just forget our names."

She knew the exact moment the resolve in his hazel eyes crumbled. His handsome features softened, his head tilted toward her. Their lips were inches apart. Lana's heart did a crazy lurch. She wanted this man. She might be insane for that, probably still in shock, most likely about to make another huge mistake.

But she still wanted him.

She bridged the distance between their lips and kissed him. It was supposed to be a soft kiss, an exploratory brushing of mouths, but what it ended up being was…pure passion. Deacon fused his mouth to hers, kissing her so deeply he stole the breath from her lungs. His tongue slid into her mouth, seeking hers, sending little bursts of heat to her core.

No stopping it. One second they were sitting side by side, kissing wildly, the next she was flat on her back, her torn sweater yanked up to her chin, with Deacon's tongue on her breasts. His body was heavy on top of hers, the weight of him bringing both a thrill and a sense of security.

Pleasure cascaded through her body as he lavished attention on her breasts, which were full and achy beneath his lips. Not to mention extremely sensitive, thanks to the pregnancy. She moaned as he suckled one beaded nipple, the excitement rising inside her so strongly she lifted her hips so she could rub herself against him. The feel of his massive erection only fueled the excitement.

When Deacon latched his mouth onto her other breast, her hips bucked again and another desperate cry slipped from her lips. He instantly pulled back. "Am I hurting you?" he asked roughly.

"No, it feels good," she whispered. "Everything you're doing feels so good."

Looking appeased, he resumed his gentle assault, kissing and fondling her breasts, running his big hands over her hips. And then one hand moved between her legs, stroking her over her pants, teasing and rubbing until she impatiently fumbled for the button at her waistband.

Deacon helped her out, popping open the button and sliding the material down her legs. His hand returned to tease her throbbing sex, and somehow he managed to remove every last inch of clothing separating them—using only one hand. His shirt and pants wound up on the floor, her bra disappeared entirely, and his boxers and her panties were a tangled mess at their feet.

They both groaned as his bare chest met her breasts. The light dusting of hair between his pecs tickled her rigid nipples, making Lana giddy with desire. They kissed again, while his heavy erection strained against her belly. Lana reached down, stroked him, pumped him, drawing a ragged groan from his lips. Flames of arousal licked at her skin, heating that tender spot between her legs, until she finally brought his tip there and teased them both.

She almost reminded him to get protection, but suddenly they both glanced down at her stomach, and the realization that they didn't need anything seemed to settle over both of them. Bracing his hands on her waist, Deacon pushed himself inside her. He dragged out the motion, sliding in slowly, inch by incredible inch.

Sweat bloomed on Lana's forehead. This was *torture.* She wanted him to fill her, to drive her over the edge into oblivion. With an impatient moan, she lifted her bottom, joining their bodies completely.

Deacon's head fell against her neck, his groan warming her skin. He withdrew slightly, and then he was moving. A fast, reckless pace that had her clinging to his strong back. Pleasure swelled in her womb, rising, spreading. Every muscle in her body tightened, every nerve ending sizzled with her impending climax.

And then Deacon squeezed out, *"Lana,"* and she toppled right over that edge. Her climax ripped through her, so raw and powerful that her fingernails dug into the sinewy muscles of his back. Deacon's hazel eyes burned with arousal, glazed with release, and his guttural cry and hurried thrusts intensified the waves of pleasure crashing through her body.

When the waves finally ebbed, delicious lethargy spread through her. Deacon's chest rose and fell against her breasts, his breath hot on her neck, his lips even hotter as he peppered kisses on her skin.

"God, Lana," he murmured. "You're so incredible."

She waited for her pulse to slow, for her limbs to figure out how to move again and then she rolled over to her side so they lay face to face.

"I like seeing you look like this," she murmured back, as she traced the proud line of his jaw with her thumb.

"Like what?"

"Not so...*hard.*" She touched his fuller bottom lip. "Not so cold."

He rested one hand on her waist, drawing circles over her hip bone with one lazy finger. "It only happens when I'm around you."

The gruff confession brought a spark of gratification. "I guess that makes me pretty special."

"More than you'll ever know."

Their gazes locked, and then, as if pulled by a magnet, they both looked down at her belly again.

"I didn't hurt you, did I?" he asked, the concern in his voice making her heart do a little flip.

"You didn't hurt me," she assured him. "Or the baby."

To her disappointment, the softness in his eyes dimmed at the mention of their child. Her throat tightened as a crushing realization pressed against her chest.

"You're not planning on being in this baby's life, are you?"

His shuttered expression was all the answer she needed.

"Why?" she whispered.

"Because I can't."

"Why?" She knew she sounded like a two-year-old tossing "whys" at her parents, but she truly couldn't make sense of any of this. "We got away, Deacon. Nobody has to know you were ever involved in the abduction. We could—" Her voice cracked. "We could raise this baby together."

Pure torture reflected in his eyes. "I'll know, Lana. *I'll* always know that I was responsible for keeping you hostage. And I can't live with that. I can't be with you knowing how much pain I caused."

His words settled between them like an impassable mountain. She knew then that no matter how much she argued, how much she tried to show him otherwise, she might never be able to break through that obstacle. His guilt. His shame.

"I'm going to get you back to your family," he went on, his voice husky, "and then I'll disappear from your life. I know that's not what you want to hear, but—"

"What happened after your parents died?" she cut in.

He flinched, as if the question caused physical pain.

"Tell me," she pressed.

"I…survived."

Those three little syllables told her so much more than he'd probably intended to reveal. "How?" she asked.

He shifted, his pecs flexing from the movement. "However I could. I ran drugs for a couple of guys in South Boston. Did some enforcer work for the Southie mafia."

"Enforcer work?"

"I beat up lowlifes who owed them money," he said flatly.

A short silence fell. Lana suspected that was all she'd get from him, but to her surprise, he continued. His expression never changed, but the pain in his tone hung in the air.

"We were wealthy. Did I tell you that?"

"No, you didn't."

"Well, it's true. Disgustingly wealthy, in fact. My father owned a shipping company, he inherited it from his father, who inherited it from *his* father. The family business was worth billions."

Lana blinked in shock. She was no stranger to family money, but somehow she couldn't picture Deacon growing up with such affluence.

"Mom was a renowned ballerina in her time," he went on, a faraway note entering his voice. "She was so beautiful, unbelievably graceful. She retired after she had me, but she still kept a dance studio on the top floor of our house. I used to sit there and watch her dance for hours."

"And your dad?"

"He wasn't as gentle as my mother. He… I guess you could call him abusive."

"He hit her?"

"No. He didn't use fists, he used words. He wanted so much from everyone, from her, from me, and we always came up short. We always disappointed him, and he never hesitated to tell us that, especially her. And then one day, he just snapped." Deacon's voice thickened with pain. "I don't know why. I have no clue what led to it, what she might have said or done to trigger him. I hired a PI about fifteen years ago, trying to piece it together, but he came up with nothing. Mom wasn't cheating, hadn't planned on leaving, hadn't done *anything*. My father just..."

He stopped abruptly. Lana knew what came next, a tragic murder-suicide that had shattered Deacon's entire world. Rather than focus on that horrifying snippet of history, she said, "After they died, what happened to the money?"

"My uncle happened." Bitterness dripped from the admission. "I was only fifteen, so he became my guardian. He would run the business until I came of age, but what he did was run it into the ground. He also threw me out."

She sucked in a breath. "Why would he do that?"

"Greed," Deacon said emphatically. "He was

always so envious of my father. Their father had favored his eldest, and my uncle James was the son who got hand-me-downs and leftovers. James was bitter. He also had a massive gambling problem and piss-poor business sense. He got rid of me, and then managed to lose every last penny his ancestors had worked so hard to earn."

The picture Deacon painted was so awful Lana reached out to touch his chest. She pressed her palm to his heart, feeling each erratic beat rapping against her flesh. "Where did you go?"

"Wherever I could make money."

She hesitated. "Have you kidnapped other people before?"

"A few. Not to be callous, but most of them deserved it. Normally I'm hired for mercenary work—raiding villages, extracting relief workers from hot areas. Sometimes the jobs are legal, other times they aren't."

His reply offered no apology, and Lana wasn't sure it deserved one. She suddenly imagined a fifteen-year-old Deacon living on the streets, scrounging to feed and clothe himself. She couldn't even fathom how he'd managed to survive. She'd been fortunate enough to grow up with financially secure parents who loved and cherished her. What would she have done if her parents died and Uncle Donald had disowned her? Would she have turned to a dangerous lifestyle the way Deacon had?

"And you survived," she said quietly, stroking the hot skin of his chest. "Whatever you did in the past ensured you stayed alive. But now..."

"But now nothing. I may have survived, but my choices have pretty much sucked every last drop of humanity out of me, Lana."

"I don't believe that."

"It's true." His hand covered hers, slowly removing her fingers from his skin. "I have nothing to give to a child, a wife. There's no goodness left in me, and you, our *baby,* deserve a good life."

"You *are* good," she disagreed. "You protected us this whole time. You kept us alive. How can you not see that?"

With methodical motions, he disentangled himself from their embrace and rose from the bed. His nudity brought a spark of desire, which fizzled the second he continued speaking.

"You deserve more than I could ever give you," he said hoarsely. "And your family will give you everything I can't. They'll help you take care of this baby. They'll make sure nothing bad ever happens to either of you."

My family can't be a father to this child, she wanted to argue, but the objection got stuck in her throat. He wouldn't hear it anyway. Deacon Holt had obviously decided what kind of man he was years ago, and nothing she could say was going to sway him.

As he bent down to retrieve his boxers, she stared at the sleek, sculpted lines of his body, the classically handsome planes of his face. She could see it now, his upbringing, his roots. He might deny it, but he'd inherited his mother's grace, his father's polish.

And maybe nothing she said would get through to him, she thought, as she watched him get dressed, but perhaps words weren't the solution here. Perhaps what she really needed to do was *show* him. Show him that he did indeed have some decency left inside him. Show him that he wasn't a robot, but a living, breathing human being with a capacity for greatness.

A man strong enough to be a father to their baby.

Captain Jim Kelley had just hopped into one of the nondescript Town Cars of the security detail when a satellite phone was thrust into his hands. The soldier who handed him the phone wore a blank look, shrugging as if to say, *I have no clue what's up.*

Stifling a sigh, Jim signaled for the driver to go and raised the phone to his ear. "Captain Kelley," he barked.

"Kelley," came Colonel Keaton's sharp voice.

Jim's sigh reached the surface. Damn. This didn't sound good. He hoped the colonel wasn't sending Delta Company on a last-second assignment or something. Jim and his crew had just spent the past two weeks providing additional security to the Secretary of Defense, who'd been meeting with various South American leaders to discuss the arms trade. He'd been looking forward to heading back to his Georgetown home, cracking open a cold beer and sitting on the couch for a few days.

The colonel's next words, however, sent a flicker of surprise through him. "I've got your mother on the line. I'm patching her through."

And then Keaton's voice faded and was replaced by his mother's urgent, "Jim, are you there?"

Jim instantly tensed. A few days ago, one of the men in Delta Company had been messing around on the internet and had discovered a weeks-old news article about Jim's father. About the fact that *six* women had come forward claiming to be Senator Kelley's mistresses. As expected, Jim had been livid, but he hadn't had a chance to call his mother. Now, hearing her voice, that anger returned full force.

"I'm here." His voice cracked slightly. "I heard what happened, Mom. I'm so sorry."

She gasped. "You know about Lana?"

"Lana?" Unease crawled up his spine. "I was referring to Dad."

"Oh."

"What are *you* talking about? What's happened to Lana?"

"She's gone, Jimmy." An unmistakable sob ripped through the line.

Jim's entire body went frozen with shock. His sister was *gone?* What the hell did that mean? He listened as his mother cried on the other end, fear rising inside him.

"Mom, what do you mean she's gone? Where is she?" For a second, he wondered if Lana had done something crazy, like hop a plane to

Africa to help children with AIDS. He could totally see her doing that. Lana's heart was bigger than a small country, and despite her sweet disposition, she did get stubborn and wild every now and then.

But apparently not now, he realized in dismay, as his mother said, "She's been kidnapped."

Jim felt lightheaded. "What?"

He could barely keep up with his mother's panic-driven words, but he got the gist of it. Lana had disappeared in Paris and was being held hostage by Hank Kelley's enemies. Relief coursed through him when his mother explained that Hank had spoken to Lana several times, but the relief transformed into rage when she described the DVD and photograph that had been delivered to the ranch.

"But she's alive," he ground out, sheer fury coating his throat like sulfuric acid.

"We think so," his mother said with an anguished whimper. "Cole deduced from the video that she might be in D.C., but we're not sure. And then last night there were reports of gunfire in a neighborhood near Stanton Park. Federal agents searched every inch of the neighborhood and didn't find a thing. Jimmy, we don't know where she is."

His mother's distress was like a knife to the heart. He'd always done his best to keep his mom happy, especially since his father didn't seem interested in doing so, but right now, he felt totally and completely helpless.

"There's more," his mother added. "The kidnappers called again, and they want to set up an exchange."

"Money?"

"No. They want your *father*. I've been trying to get through to you for days now. I don't know what to do. I don't trust these people, and I'm beginning to think they're never going to let my baby go. Nothing about this exchange makes sense, Jimmy."

"You're right."

Everything his mother had just told him succeeded in heightening the anger rolling in his gut. Of course this was about his father. Hank Kelley's recklessness and insensitivity was always at the root of every problem this family ever encountered.

"Where is Dad now?" he asked coldly.

"Maple Cove. He's staying with Cole." Sarah paused. "People are trying to kill him."

Jim almost muttered "good," but quickly tamped down the cruel thought. He didn't want to see his father dead. No matter how much heartache Hank Kelley had caused over the years, he was still Jim's father.

And, as a dutiful son, he was going to come home and clean up his daddy's mess.

"Are you at the mansion?" he asked his mother.

"No, I'm staying at Vivienne's house in Martha's Vineyard."

"Good. Stay there. And as of this moment, I'm arranging for a guard to come stay with you." Before she could protest, he hurried on in a brisk tone. "I'll fly to Maple Cove tonight. I'll take care of everything, okay, Mom?"

"Just be careful. Please, promise to take care of yourself."

"I will." His jaw hardened. "And don't worry, I'm going to find Lana and bring her home."

Among other things…

He decided not to mention that. His mother was distraught enough as it was. No need to worry her further.

But he had no intention of letting this end simply with Lana's safe return. Because nobody, *nobody,* was going to kidnap his sister and live to tell about it.

Jim would make sure of that.

Chapter 13

Deacon and Lana reached Cleveland in the late afternoon, and by the time he pulled into the parking lot of the motel, he was dying to get out of the car. Lana's attempts at making conversation had begun to make him unbelievably uncomfortable. Ever since he'd poured out his life story to her while they lay in bed, he'd tried to keep some distance between them. Kept his responses short, forced himself not to touch her. Yet Lana seemed determined to claw her way through his self-imposed distance.

And he knew why. Somehow she'd convinced herself that he was capable of being a father to this kid. She truly believed they might have some sort of future together.

Deacon knew better, though. Even if he weren't on the wrong side of the law and would probably be arrested when this was all over, he didn't belong in Lana's life. He didn't belong anywhere.

The motel he'd found was located on the out-skirts of the city, near an industrial area where every company name seemed to have the word *mega* in it. Mega Steel Corporation, Mega Shutters, Megapaint, Inc. Considering the min-iscule size of the buildings, *mega* seemed ab-surdly hyperbolic.

"Do you think there's a mega sandwich shop around here? Because I'm mega hungry," Lana murmured.

His lips twitched. Although she'd claimed in her endless chattering during the six-hour drive that she didn't have a great sense of humor, he found himself amused by her wry remarks and subtle jokes. He'd had to stifle several chuckles already. That would have defeated the purpose of distance.

"I'll grab us something from the café I spotted around the corner," he said.

They entered the motel room, which was as shabby as the one they'd spent last night in. Lana removed the oversize flannel shirt he'd given her, which left her in the oversize sweater that hung past the knees of her snug black track pants. The bloodstained sweater she'd worn yesterday had been tossed out, and since Deacon had neglected to bring her suitcase when they escaped the apartment, she now had no choice but to wear his clothes.

For some reason, the sight of her slender body covered in his shirts brought a strange spark of satisfaction.

Lana's blue eyes zeroed in on the telephone sitting on the splintered cedar nightstand. "Can I call my parents?" she asked softly.

Regret lined his tone. "I'm afraid not."

She met his gaze. "Why not?"

"Le Clair probably bugged their phones. Or maybe not. Either way, we can't take the chance that he or his men will be listening to the calls."

"But what if I don't reveal our location? I can just say I got away and I'm making my way home."

He shook his head. "We still might be tracked here. If the phones are bugged, Le Clair will get a trace and find us." When her face fell, he let out a breath. "I know you want to speak to your family, but just hold on a bit longer. You'll be home soon."

"When?"

"A few days, if we drive without making too many stops. But I want to get an early start in the morning so we can make it to Chicago at a decent time. There's someone I need to see."

Suspicion clouded her face. "Who?"

"An old friend of mine. We worked on a couple of assignments together in the Middle East."

"Wait, you have a friend?"

She sounded so surprised he felt a prickle of

irritation. "Even bad guys like me have friends." He suddenly sighed. "Well, O'Neal's more of an acquaintance, actually."

Lana seemed to be fighting a laugh. "Okay. So why do we need to see this acquaintance?"

"We need money. Ammo. A vehicle I won't need to ditch every six hours."

"Are you sure we can trust this guy?"

"We have no choice," he said quietly. "We won't make it to Montana without supplies."

"All right. If you think it's safe."

He almost cringed. She gave her trust to him so freely, without any hesitation. That unfailing idealism again, her need to seek out the best in everyone.

Discomfort curled in his stomach. Sometimes he wished she'd just hate him. Distrust him. Those were responses he'd become accustomed to, reactions he expected from those around him. Lana's determination to ignore the darkness inside him was something he didn't quite know how to handle.

He cleared his throat. "I'll go grab us some food. Lock the door behind me." As an after-thought, he unzipped the duffel bag he'd set on the bed, retrieved a black .35 mm and held it out to her. "Keep this close."

Leaving the room, he headed to the car and made a quick trip to the coffee shop, where he purchased several sandwiches, some cookies, coffee for himself and juice for Lana. When he got back to the motel, Lana was sitting in the tiny kitchenette flipping through a newspaper that must have been left there by the previous occupant.

The frown marring her face told him the news wasn't good. "What's up?" he asked, gesturing to the paper.

"My dad." Her tone was flat as she held up one page in particular.

Senator's Extracurricular Activities, the head-line read. Next to the article was a photograph of Hank Kelley's distinguished features, a smug smile on his face. Across from Kelley was a second photo, this one showcasing the striking face of a redhead in her mid- to late-twenties. One of Kelley's mistresses apparently.

"How could he do this?" Lana mumbled, more to herself than him. He understood her distress—hearing the news was one thing, but seeing the photos was like a punch to the gut. "God, seeing this makes me…it makes me…"

"Angry?" Deacon supplied, handing her one of the plastic-wrapped sandwiches.

"Yeah." Shock filled her face. "Yes," she said in a raised voice. "I *am* angry."

The look in her eyes revealed such disbelief, such startled confusion, that he had to fight another smile. "That's not an emotion you feel often, is it?"

She slowly shook her head. "No. I've never really seen the point in getting ticked off about things. Besides, my dad isn't a bad person. He's made a lot of mistakes, sure, but he's like a little kid, you know? So full of life and mischief and he's…" She halted abruptly.

Deacon raised the coffee cup to his lips and took a long swallow, waiting for her to continue. He got the feeling he might be witnessing an epiphany here. And not the good kind.

"Selfish," she finally burst out, her blue eyes blazing. "He's selfish, Deacon! He cheated on my mother with who knows how many women! He's let down each one of my brothers, on numerous occasions. He's…" Her voice lowered to an anguished whisper. "He's let *me* down."

His chest squeezed at the forlorn expression that crossed her beautiful face.

"And I always forgave him. I always ignored everything he did." She stared at him, suddenly looking beaten. "How can I ignore it now?"

"You can't." He sank into one of the plastic chairs at the tiny table. "You just stop putting him on a pedestal and recognize that he's flawed. Jeez, Lana, *everyone* is flawed."

She didn't respond to the frank statement. Or maybe she'd simply chosen not to hear it. He noticed her hands tremble slightly as she unwrapped the sandwich and took a small bite. She chewed, then made a face.

"This tastes like sandpaper," she remarked, but continued eating nonetheless.

Deacon dug into his own sandwich and had to agree with her assessment. "Definitely bland," he agreed. "Too bad this room doesn't have a full kitchen. I would've made you something else."

"You know, you still haven't told me where you learned to cook so well."

"Culinary camp," he said lightly.

Her blond eyebrows rose. "Seriously?"

"My parents made sure I had a well-rounded education." He sipped his coffee again. "Cooking lessons, dance lessons, language classes, sports, literary clubs. I was probably the most overeducated teenager on the planet."

"And yet…"

Her voice drifted, and he instantly stiffened. "And yet I became a criminal?" he finished callously.

She hesitated for a moment. "I understand you had to do whatever you could survive when you were younger, but you could have gone back to school at some point. Finished your education. Gotten a job."

"I suppose I could have scribbled *drug dealer* under previous employment," he agreed sardonically.

Irritation flashed in her eyes. "You don't have to be an ass. I'm just pointing out you had other options."

"Not back then." His jaw tightened. "And not now. At some point I took the wrong turn, and it's too late to take a different path now. I am who I am, Lana. I can't rewrite history, and I can't magically become the man you think I should be."

"The man you *want* to be," she corrected. "Don't deny it. I've seen the shame in your eyes, when you think you're masking it. This has nothing to do with me, or what I want. This is all you, Deacon. *You* don't like what you do."

With a dainty shrug, she resumed eating, alternating between munching on cookies and taking little sips of the orange juice he'd brought her. Deacon's appetite left him, as he sat there in silence, thinking about what she'd said.

Was this the life he wanted for himself? Growing up, he'd had big dreams—going to college, running the family business, maybe starting up his own company.

Growing up, he'd also had the means to do those things.

You have them now, too.

He reached for his cup, needing caffeine to fuel his rampant thoughts. Yeah, he did have the means now. Money. Plenty of time.

He quickly shoved aside the foolish notions running through his mind. Jeez, Lana's hope-springs-eternal attitude was beginning to infect him. To cloud his judgment.

What the hell else would he do with his life? He was good at being a soldier of fortune. Great at it, actually. Those silly childhood dreams of his had been squashed years ago. They weren't viable options any longer.

And he needed to remember that.

"Are you sure you can trust this guy?" Lana asked for the tenth time as she hovered behind Deacon's broad back.

They were climbing a narrow stairwell up to Shane O'Neal's apartment, and Lana hadn't been able to fight her unease since the moment they'd arrived in Chicago. It didn't help that O'Neal lived above a gun store, which he apparently owned and ran. She stuck close to Deacon, wrinkling her nose at the musty stench in the air.

"Yes, we can trust him," Deacon answered for the tenth time. He glanced at her over his shoulder. "We'll be in and out, okay? Ten minutes tops."

They reached the top of the stairs and paused in front of a weathered wooden door that swung open before they could knock. Deacon had discreetly pointed out one of the cameras at the bottom of the stairwell, so O'Neal knew they were here. Apparently Deacon's "friend" took security very seriously.

Not his appearance, though, Lana noticed, as she laid eyes on the man Deacon claimed to trust. Shane O'Neal had scruffy reddish-brown hair that came down to his shoulders and an unkempt beard that devoured his entire face. He wore camo pants with a red stain on the knee— she hoped it wasn't blood—and a black T-shirt that boasted at least six holes in various places.

His pale blue eyes were sharp, however, out of sync with his couch-potato looks.

"Were you followed?" was the first thing O'Neal asked in a faint Irish brogue.

Deacon shook his head.

"Good." The door opened wider. "Come in."

Lana's eyed widened as she got a good look at the interior of O'Neal's flat. There was a surprisingly spacious living area, made all the more spacious by the complete lack of furniture in it. No chairs, couches, coffee table. Evidently O'Neal didn't spend much time here, unless he came in to admire the vast amount of rifles hanging on one entire wall. The adjacent wall featured a collection of swords. Pleasant guy.

O'Neal led them down a corridor lit only by a bare bulb dangling from the ceiling. They passed two doors, both closed, and finally entered a large room filled with computer monitors, metal shelving and enormous steel crates.

"So is this your girl?" O'Neal asked in an indifferent voice as he moved toward a metal file cabinet jammed between two computer desks.

"A friend," Deacon answered vaguely. "Lana, meet Shane. Shane, Lana."

She managed a faint hello, all the while irritated by Deacon's introduction. A friend? Try the mother of his unborn child! Obviously her numerous attempts at conversational connections had failed miserably. He seemed just as determined to keep her at arm's length. To de-

posit her on her family's doorstep and disappear from her life.

O'Neal pulled a fat manila envelope from the cabinet. "I assume this will do?"

Deacon took the envelope and peered inside. Lana craned her neck, raising a brow when she caught a quick glimpse of the thick stack of bills. She forced herself not to ask why O'Neal had huge envelopes of money lying around the house. She wasn't sure she wanted to know anyway.

The men didn't say much as O'Neal proceeded to open a crate and rummage through a scary amount of ammunition clips. "Still using the .35 mm?" O'Neal asked.

Deacon nodded. "And the .45."

O'Neal tossed a dozen clips into a small black shoulder bag, then handed it to Deacon. "Where you headed?" he asked, not sounding too interested.

"Montana," Lana said before she could stop herself.

She immediately got a dark scolding look from Deacon. Shoot. She shouldn't have revealed their destination. Deacon might trust this man, but he'd specifically told her in the car not to offer any details.

"And then Oregon," she added belatedly. "My family has a house on the coast."

"Uh-huh," O'Neal said, unconcerned.

At least he didn't seem to care one way or the other where they were heading. This entire *friendship* was kind of baffling. These two men had worked together on several assignments, yet they acted like complete strangers. And O'Neal was just handing Deacon money and ammo like they were Tic-Tacs. Without even questioning it.

"I got the car, too," O'Neal told Deacon. He reached into his pocket and extracted a set of keys. "It's parked out back. Blue pickup."

"Thanks." Deacon put his hand on Lana's arm and took a sideways step to the door. "I owe you, man."

"And I'll collect," O'Neal said, grinning for the first time since they arrived.

"I wouldn't expect anything less."

And then, just like that, they were ushered to the front door, saying goodbye and descending the mildew-scented stairwell again.

"That's it?" Lana hissed.

"Like I said, in and out," Deacon replied with a shrug.

She remained dumbfounded. "Yeah, but…he gave us all that money, the bullets, the car, without even asking what we needed it for."

"That's how it works. The mercenary community is fairly tight-knit. You're in a jam, a fellow soldier will bail you out, no questions asked. And then you return the favor."

They rounded the building toward the gravel lot in the back, and sure enough, a dark blue pickup waited for them.

"So you don't help each other out of the goodness of your hearts?" she asked, slightly confused.

The corner of his mouth lifted. "You're assuming we have hearts, sweetheart." He clicked on the car remote to unlock the doors.

Lana bit the inside of her cheek as she slid into the passenger seat. She didn't understand this world. These people. When she helped someone, she didn't expect anything in return. She did it because she genuinely wanted to make things better for the other person. In Deacon's world, however, nothing came free. Or cheap.

She suddenly experienced a burst of guilt, wondering what Shane O'Neal would demand of Deacon in exchange for this afternoon's encounter.

"I forgot, I got you something when we made that pit stop in South Bend," Deacon said after he started the engine.

Surprise slid through her. "You did?"

He twisted his big body around and rummaged through the duffel he'd tossed in the backseat, turning a moment later with a small pill bottle in his hand. Looking awkward, he handed it to her.

Lana stared down at the label, battling between shock and pure joy. Prenatal vitamins. He'd actually bought her prenatal vitamins. Did that mean… Was he beginning to come around about the baby?

"Thank you," she murmured, her chest tight with emotion.

He shrugged. "I figured you'd need 'em."

She curled her fingers around the pill bottle, suddenly needing to cling to it. Maybe the tender gesture didn't have any deeper meaning. Maybe he'd only done it to make himself feel better, to know she'd be taking care of herself after he disappeared from her life.

But she couldn't help thinking that it *did* mean something. That Deacon had indeed heard everything she'd been saying and was finally beginning to see that his future could hold so much more than he'd always believed. Not just his future, but *their* future.

The impulsive notion gave her pause. She fixed her gaze out the window, watching the scenery on Lakeshore Drive whiz past. She suddenly had to ask herself exactly what she wanted from this man. To simply be a father to their child? Or did she want more?

She closed her eyes, a barrage of images swirling through her brain. She imagined Deacon's strong arms gently cradling their baby, his rugged face soft with emotion. Deacon talking gruffly to their baby, looking down with pride.

And then the fantasy took a different turn. She pictured herself waking up every morning with her head pressed against Deacon's rock-hard chest. Whispering to each other as they fell asleep in each other's arms. Sitting at the kitchen table while he cooked for her.

Her eyelids snapped open. Oh, lord. This wasn't just about the baby. This was about her. About *them*.

"Oh, my God," she blurted out.

Deacon sharply swiveled his head. "What's wrong?"

She swallowed hard, searching for her voice. "Nothing," she finally said. "I just never realized how beautiful the view of the lake is."

His brows furrowed, as if he didn't quite believe her, or know how to respond. Eventually he just shrugged. "Yeah, it's pretty nice, I guess."

Lana glued her gaze to the window again, trying to actually focus on the lake this time in the hope of erasing the terrifying thought that had crashed into her head before her outburst.

But it was impossible to erase. It lingered in her brain, making her a little lightheaded and a lot confused.

Was it possible?

Was she actually falling in love with Deacon Holt?

Chapter 14

Jim Kelley was feeling irritable as hell as he killed the engine of the pickup he'd rented at the airport and stared at the pale yellow glow seeping from the floor-to-ceiling windows of his brother's ranch house. In the distance, the mountains dominated the horizon, their snow-dusted peaks like majestic castle turrets in the sky. Normally the sheer beauty of the landscape soothed Jim's soul. As a kid he used to prowl the hills and trails of the property, astride his favorite dun-colored mare, Heidi.

Tonight, though, the mountains only served as a reminder of the towering obstacles in his path. He'd called every contact imaginable on the plane ride here, and hadn't come up with a single lead regarding Lana's whereabouts. Many of the contacts he phoned didn't even know that Lana was missing. Apparently Hank had kept the story out of the press for as long as he could, and the news had only broken a couple of days ago. Jim had encountered more than a dozen reporters milling at the gates of the Bar Lazy K. They'd surrounded his truck like vultures, eager to scavenge any details they could about Lana's disappearance or the senator's misdeeds. At ten o'clock at night. Christ, didn't those people have anything better to do?

Jim slowly uncurled his fingers from the steering wheel and got out of the truck. His boots connected with the dusty earth, kicking up little clouds as he headed for the porch. He entered the ranch house without knocking, and his ears immediately perked at the sound of muffled voices drifting from the doorway of the great room.

He made a beeline for it, throwing open the heavy doors without a care of what he'd find on the other side. What he found, though, startled the hell out of him. His father sat on one edge of the sofa, holding a highball glass filled to the rim with bourbon. Standing near the bookshelf was Gage Prescott, his dad's bodyguard, but it wasn't the sight of Gage that threw Jim for a loop. It was his brother Cole, who was plopped down on the other end of the couch, a beer in hand.

Cole *willingly* sitting with their father?

Jim resisted the urge to shake the confusion from his head. Had hell frozen over?

Three heads jerked up at his abrupt entrance.

"Jim?" Hank said in surprise, the sudden shift of his body causing the ice cubes in his glass to clink together like marbles.

Jim didn't bother with pleasantries. "What the *hell* have you done?"

Hank flinched as if he'd been shot. A stunned silence descended on the room.

"Your mother told you about Lana," Hank finally said in a resigned voice.

"She did," Jim confirmed coldly. "I shouldn't be surprised that you didn't call me yourself. You've always let Mom clean up your messes."

The barb got him another flinch, along with a surprising frown from Cole. "Cool it, Jimmy." Cole set his beer bottle on the coffee table and slowly got to his feet, squaring the broad shoulders of his six-foot frame.

"You're defending him?" Jim said in disbelief.

His brother sighed. "Trust me, we've all given him a lot of grief over the past couple of months. It's nothing he hasn't heard before."

Jim shook his head, a wave of frustration swelling in his gut. "And he should keep hearing it," he shot back. "Christ! What are you guys doing, sitting around sipping on beer and bourbon? Lana is out there somewhere! Alone. *Scared.* Why isn't this place crawling with Feds?"

"A couple of agents are coming tomorrow morning," Cole explained in a low voice. "They're coordinating the exchange."

Jim went momentarily speechless. "Exchange?"

He hissed out a breath, turning to his father. "Mom was right. You're planning on sacrificing yourself for Lana."

His father stared at him with remorseful eyes. "Do I have any other choice?"

"Yes," Jim snapped. "You stay out of it and let the Feds do their thing. Have you offered the kidnappers a ransom?"

"They don't want one." Gage spoke from his perch by the bookshelf.

"They want Dad," Cole answered flatly.

"Why?" Jim ran a hand through his dark hair. "What the hell is going on here?"

The three men exchanged somewhat cryptic looks, and then Cole let out a heavy breath. "You might as well sit down, little brother. This will probably take a while."

"I'm not sure I like being on the run," Lana declared as she stepped out of yet another miniscule bathroom, Deacon's T-shirt sagging down to her knees.

Deacon glanced up from the brochure he was reading and offered a wry look. "Not quite as exciting as the movies portray, huh?"

"You got that right."

After three days of non-stop driving, and three nights in motels that only seemed to get more dilapidated, Lana longed for her brother's house in Maple Cove, for the mouthwatering scent of Hannah's cooking. Even more, she wanted to hear a familiar voice, but Deacon repeatedly warned her it could be dangerous if they contacted any member of her family. Fortunately, they didn't have much farther to go. Tomorrow morning they'd make the nine-hour drive to Maple Cove, and by tomorrow night, she'd be with her family. Safe and sound.

And Deacon would be gone.

"Did you know there's a Steamboat Warehouse near here?" Deacon asked, holding up the tourism pamphlet he'd taken from the motel lobby. "It was built in 1883."

She bent over to towel-dry her wet hair, peeking out from under the towel to scowl at him. "Gee, that sounds so exciting. Please take me there, Deacon."

He laughed.

Lana nearly dropped the towel. He'd actually laughed. Ever since the night they'd made love, she'd noticed him making a tiresome effort to remain aloof. He spoke in short sentences, avoided her eyes whenever he could, slept on the floor every night.

And although his detachment annoyed her, it had also given her time to think about the shocking realization she'd reached in the truck the other day. The whole *L*-word dilemma. She'd finally decided that she was being silly. Of course she wasn't falling for Deacon. So what if the sex had been out of this world? So what if she melted just a little each time he smiled or laughed or showed a sliver of emotion?

That didn't mean she was falling in love with him. It just meant she liked him. Which was totally natural. A woman ought to like the father of her baby, right?

She finished drying her hair, then headed into the bathroom to hang the towel on the rack. Just as she came out, Deacon was coming in. Their bodies collided, sending an instant jolt of heat through her. Her nipples tightened against the material of her shirt, a reaction that Deacon didn't fail to notice.

"I…was going to hop in the shower," he said roughly.

She swallowed. "Okay."

Neither of them made a move to pull back from the chest-to-chest contact. Her breasts swelled, growing heavy with need at the feel of his defined pecs pressed against them.

"Uh…" Deacon trailed off.

Their eyes locked. Awareness sizzled between them like an electric current.

Then he coughed, and painstakingly moved back. "Uh, yeah, a shower."

Disappointment flooded her belly as he side-stepped her and walked into the bathroom. A moment later, the door quietly closed. She heard the faucet creak and the sound of rushing water met her ears.

With a ragged breath, she stepped away from the door and slid under the ugly checkered bedspread, trying to get comfortable in bed. Her hands moved to her belly, stroking it gently. It was probably for the best. Giving in to her attraction to Deacon again wouldn't lead to anything anyway. He'd made it glaringly obvious that he wasn't going to stick around. He was simply making amends for the ordeal she'd been through, taking her back to her family as a form of reparation.

Her attempts to get him to open up continually failed. Every subtle nudge, every little reminder that there was hope for his future, had gone unnoticed.

Sex wasn't going to bring him around. It would only complicate things further, add to the tangled knot of confusing emotions already lodged inside her.

At the mere thought of sex, though, hot flames of arousal licked every inch of her suddenly feverish skin.

"Snap out of it," she muttered to herself.

Right. She had to get a grip. She couldn't sleep with Deacon again.

It was a bad idea.

A mistake.

But…

But just one more time wouldn't hurt, right?

Lana was naked when Deacon walked into the bedroom.

He had to do a double-take to be sure, but yup, naked. She lay on top of the frayed blanket, her pale skin shimmering in the dim lighting of the room. His mouth instantly went dry. His pulse kicked off in a gallop.

He couldn't tear his eyes from her. Her round breasts, tipped by beaded pink nipples. Her firm thighs and shapely legs, the delicate arch of her feet. His gaze rested on her belly, and his heart did a strange lurch when he noticed the tiny bump. There was a baby in there. *His* baby.

Christ.

"What are you doing?" he choked out, suddenly wishing he'd taken all his clothes into the bathroom instead of just a pair of black boxers. His body's reaction was not one she'd fail to notice. His erection hung hot and heavy between his legs, straining against his boxers.

"I'm waiting for you to join me."

"Lana." He gulped. "You know this isn't a good idea."

"Sure it is." She shot a pointed look at his groin. "And I think you know it, too."

How could he argue with that? How could he explain that although his body was raring to go, his brain was screaming for him to get dressed and walk out the door? A part of him wished he could. Just cut and run, let Lana make it back to her family on her own, so he could leave the country and forget he'd ever met her.

But he couldn't do that. The sheer thought of leaving her sent waves of agony roaring through him.

He stood there frozen in place, torn between marching back to the bathroom or climbing into bed with her. Lana apparently decided to make the decision for him, because she swung her bare legs over the side of the bed, stood up and sauntered over to him.

Wrapping her arms around his neck, she pushed her breasts into his chest. He almost keeled over with arousal.

"Lana," he began, taking one last stab at derailing this potentially destructive train.

She cut him off with a kiss.

The ability to form articulate thoughts disappeared in a sharp gust. Her lips were soft, warm, and she teased his mouth, brushing barely-there kisses over it, the tip of her tongue sweeping over his bottom lip. He instinctively parted his lips and granted her entrance, and then their tongues met and a rush of pure pleasure flooded his groin.

And just like all the other times he'd tasted her, it wasn't enough. He wanted more. *Craved* it on a raw, visceral level.

Somehow they made it to the bed, mouths and tongues fused together, hands moving and exploring, legs tangling together. Deacon was panting as he brought a hand between her thighs, as he rubbed, stroked, brought her to new levels of pleasure while she moaned against his lips. He nearly lost it when she climaxed against his palm, her core rippling and pulsing, moist and slick, while she shuddered against him.

A groan squeezed out of his chest when she encircled his shaft with warm fingers, still rocking against his hand to prolong her release. He could barely move, his muscles were taut with anticipation, but the need to be inside her broke through his lust-crazed paralysis. He covered her body with his and slid into her in one smooth glide.

He almost lost control right then, stilling her hips with his hands before she tried to move. When he looked into her eyes, the passion and acceptance he saw there nearly ripped him apart. "I won't last long," he choked out.

"I don't care," she whispered back, and lifted her bottom to fully join them together.

It was all a blur. The hurried, desperate thrusts, the feel of her fingernails digging into his back, Lana's soft voice urging him over that precipice and finally, white-hot pleasure seizing every inch of his body. He groaned into her neck, latching his mouth onto her warm flesh as release pulsed through him. He'd never felt this way with any other woman. It wasn't just the force of the climax, but something more. A tight vise around his heart that he didn't quite know how to interpret.

Kissing the side of his jaw, Lana rolled over and rested her head against his damp chest, one dainty arm slung over his abs, one leg hooked over his thighs.

Deacon stroked her blond hair and stared up at the ceiling, riddled with pain and confusion. Lana's silky tresses slid through his fingers, her breath warmed his chest. He was amazed by how small and fragile she felt in his arms, by the complete trust she offered as she nestled close to him and drifted off to sleep.

That strange and painful vise returned, squeezing tighter this time. Why did this keep happening each time he let himself get close to Lana? What *was* this?

You love her.

Deacon almost scrambled off the bed in alarm. Love? No. That was utterly illogical. He couldn't love Lana. She turned him on, sure, and she definitely inspired a powerful protective streak inside him.

But love?

Lana made a contented little sound in her

sleep and he instinctively tightened his hold on her.

I love her.

He tested the words in his mind, letting them sit, settle, develop some sort of meaning. It wouldn't be so bad, would it? Loving Lana. Protecting her, raising their kid, sharing his life with—

Out of nowhere, a grisly image slammed its way into his brain. The pool of blood surrounding his mother's long black hair. The gun dangling limply from his father's cold fingers.

Deacon sucked in a burst of oxygen, his mind reeling. Christ, who was he kidding? Of course it would be bad, loving Lana. She was the kindest person he'd ever met. Not to mention the most optimistic, smartest, prettiest... She had it all, which made his feelings for her all the more dangerous.

If he let himself love her, the darkness inside him, the darkness he'd inherited from his father, would eventually eclipse the light Lana seemed to radiate. What if he destroyed her one day, the way his mother had been destroyed?

He could never take that chance. He'd rather die first.

"Why are you so tense?"

Her concerned voice broke through the silence. She touched his chest, which was tightly constricted thanks to the breath he'd been holding.

"It's nothing," he said in a strained voice. "Go to sleep."

Her blond head lifted. Propping herself up on her elbow, she studied him with weary blue eyes, the expression revealing she knew exactly what he'd been thinking just now.

"You're not going to stick around when we get to Montana, are you, Deacon?"

He finally let out that breath. "I've been telling you that from the start."

"I know. I just hoped..."

The disappointment he heard in her soft voice almost made him backpedal. He couldn't bear hurting her, not after everything she'd been through. But he couldn't lead her on, either. She deserved much better than that.

"You hoped we could pretend I never had a hand in your kidnapping, that we'd get married and raise this kid together and live happily ever after?" He injected a note of sarcasm into the fairy tale, trying not to wince when he saw the hurt flood her face.

"Is that so far-fetched?" she whispered in the darkness.

"Yes." Slowly, he lifted her arm from his chest and tucked it against her side, then slid off the bed in search of some clothes. "It's a damned fantasy, Lana. People like you and me, we don't get together. We don't live happily ever after. *You* do, but not me."

His hands were oddly shaky as he picked up his boxers and yanked them up his thighs. Lana didn't say anything as he dressed, just lay there on her side, her blue eyes glimmering with unhappiness and some more of that disappointment.

"I still think you're wrong," she said, but this time, the conviction in her voice wavered. "You're a good man, Deacon. We can still make this work, if not for us, then at least for this baby—"

"I don't want a damned baby!" he cut in. "And I don't want to be married to a spoiled young heiress who lives in a damn dream world."

She flinched as if he'd struck her.

In that moment, he felt everything she did. The hot agony stabbing into his insides, the sorrow weighing on his chest.

He hated hurting her. He *loathed* it.

But it had to be done. She needed to face reality and understand that he was not the man for her.

Silence stretched between them like a deep abyss, and Deacon forced himself to maintain his uncaring expression. The sparkle of tears clinging to her eyelashes almost did him in, but he stayed strong. Whether she believed it or not, this was for the best. However you looked at it, his destiny led to utter destruction. Maybe he'd go to prison. Or maybe he'd die at Le Clair's enraged hands. But the biggest maybe of all, the one that had him following in his father's footsteps and hurting Lana, was one he refused to risk.

"Do you finally get it now?" he asked coldly, avoiding her tortured eyes.

"Yes," she whispered.

There was a rustling sound, and when he turned, he saw her stumbling from the bed. Without looking his way, she hurried into the bathroom and slammed the door.

You did the right thing. You protected her.

Deacon sat on the edge of the bed and rubbed his jaw with both hands, trying to cling to the confidence his brain seemed to possess.

His heart, on the other hand…well, it might need some more convincing.

Chapter 15

Lana did her best to avoid looking at Deacon during the drive to Montana. Didn't say a word, either. Because really, what was the point? He'd said everything that needed to be said last night, after he'd reached into her chest, ripped out her heart and crushed it to dust between his cruel fingers.

His words refused to leave her mind, though. *I don't want a damned baby...I don't want to be married to a spoiled young heiress who lives in a damn dream world.*

Was that truly what he thought of her? That she was spoiled? Living in a dream world? The former didn't trouble her as much as the latter. What was so wrong with believing she and Deacon could have a future? He'd rescued her from Le Clair, kept her safe this entire time and if he'd asked—heck, even if he didn't ask—she would have done everything possible to make sure he wasn't punished for his role in this abduction. He was the father of her baby, after all.

But he didn't want to be.

Glancing out the window, she focused on the mountains in the distance, but the familiar sight didn't soothe her. Soon she would be home with her family.

And soon Deacon would be gone.

"We should be there in a couple of hours."

Deacon's voice sounded rough, rusty even. He hadn't said a single word to her in eight hours.

"Uh-huh," she said dully.

She heard him let out a heavy breath. "Lana…I know you don't want to understand it, but—"

"Oh, I understand perfectly!" she interrupted. Before she could stop it, the pain and regret and anger she'd been harboring all morning exploded like a grenade. "You think I'm spoiled, you think I'm a foolish idealist, you don't give a damn about our baby and you want nothing to do with me. Is there something else I'm not understanding?"

He went deathly quiet, and she noticed the flicker of anguish in his eyes.

Good, let him be upset. "That's what I thought," she muttered.

Nearly twenty minutes passed before the excruciating silence in the vehicle was broken again.

"Damn it," Deacon swore.

She glanced over and saw him peering at the rearview mirror. Another curse hissed out of his mouth.

Alarm trickled inside her. "What's wrong?"

"We're being followed."

The stretch of highway they were on had been deserted all morning, so when Lana turned to look at the side mirror, she immediately noticed the white van behind them.

"It could be nobody," she offered.

No sooner had the words exited her mouth than the van picked up speed, now hugging their bumper.

Deacon slammed his foot on the gas pedal and the pickup hurtled forward. The van matched the pace.

"Damn," Deacon mumbled again.

Lana held her belly protectively as they sped down the two-lane road, the white van continuing its pursuit. The highway was one long stretch with no curves in the distance, but the faster Deacon drove, the more panicked Lana became. The driver behind them wasn't making any move to run them off the road, but stayed on their tail like a thoroughbred straining to close in on the front-runner.

"What do we do?" Lana demanded.

"We try to make it to the next exit and lose them then."

Deacon's plan erupted in flames as the screech of tires filled the air and a black SUV suddenly launched out from behind the white van and sped alongside them.

Heart thudding wildly, Lana peered at the windows of the SUV, but she couldn't see through the tint. Not that there was much doubt about who it was. Le Clair's men had been driving similar nondescript vehicles since they'd first abducted her.

Deacon released another wild expletive. "Get your head down," he snapped.

She obeyed instantly, ducking down and keeping her head in her lap. They hit a pothole and her butt fully lifted off the seat from the force. Deacon kept driving, flooring the gas, but the SUV beside them was faster.

Lana peeked over and her heart lodged in her throat when she saw the SUV overpower them. The wind shrieked through the window she'd left a crack open, as Deacon drove at a furious pace, and then the crunch of metal had her flying into the door. The SUV had hit them!

Deacon worked valiantly at trying to control the pickup, but the truck lurched and rocked from each vicious slam. Fear paralyzed her limbs, while her pulse drummed loudly in her ears. She wasn't sure how long Deacon would be able to keep going, and just as the thought entered her mind, the scent of burnt rubber filled her nostrils. A blur of black flew past her peripheral vision and suddenly the SUV wound up in front of them, blocking both lanes as it came to a jarring stop.

Deacon slammed on the brakes, and she would've gone flying through the windshield if not for the seat belt. But her head did connect with the glove compartment, and Lana saw stars for several long seconds. She blinked wildly, drawing in gulps of air. A car door slammed, and despite the ringing in her ears, she heard footsteps approaching their vehicle.

A second later, her door ripped open, somebody unbuckled her seat belt and she was pulled from the car and thrown into the dusty shoulder of the highway. She instantly cradled her belly rather than breaking the fall, and her forehead bounced off the gravel and sent a streak of pain through her.

A pair of black boots entered her line of vision. When she raised her head, a wave of complete misery consumed her.

"Missed me?" Le Clair asked cheerfully.

Goddamn O'Neal. As he was being hauled out of the truck, Deacon had no illusions about how Le Clair and his men had found them. Shane O'Neal had evidently given them up. Hell, the bastard had probably even put a GPS transmitter in the damn truck.

So much for the tight-knit mercenary community.

The moment Deacon's boots connected with solid ground, a fist connected with his stomach, making him double over. He glanced up to see Kilo winding his arm again, and then he gasped for air as his kidney took a vicious hit.

"That," came Le Clair's hard voice, "was for all the trouble you've caused me, Delta."

Breathing through the pain, Deacon met Le Clair's empty gray eyes. "How much?" he demanded.

"How much did it cost me to retrieve you?" Le Clair said with a knowing smile. "The original price on your head was fifty grand—I figured that would catch some attention when I spread it over the mercenary grapevine. But your friend O'Neal, I was surprised by how persuasive his negotiation skills were. We settled for seventy-five."

Seventy-five thousand bucks. Good to know how much money his fellow soldier was willing to defect for.

"More?" Kilo asked his boss in an indifferent tone, curling his fist again.

"No, we'll save the rest of Delta's punishment

for later." Le Clair clapped his hands. "Tie them up and get them in the van."

Relief rippled through him when he noticed Oscar approach with Lana. Although faint smears of blood covered her forehead, she looked unharmed. Their eyes locked, and the hurt and anger he'd seen on her face since last night had vanished, replaced with cold fear. He wished he could reassure her, but as Kilo clamped his wrists together and wrapped a thin black cord around them, Deacon knew there was nothing he could say.

They were in Le Clair's control again, and this time, there would be no escape.

"What are you going to do with us?" Lana asked in a shaky voice directed at Le Clair.

He smiled broadly. "I'm still debating the best way to kill you both. Or should I say, the most entertaining way." He nodded in approval as Oscar tightened the cord around Lana's wrists. "You've really been a pain in the ass, princess. I'm overwhelmed with anticipation at the thought of finally being rid of you."

"What about my father?" Desperation crept into her tone. "You said something about an exchange."

"Funny you should ask. We're on our way to meet your daddy right now."

The look of shock on Lana's face matched the one Deacon tried to hide. The deathly chill in his bones told him this was just another game, and Le Clair's next words confirmed it.

"Rather admirable of your father to trade his life for yours, huh, princess?" Le Clair smirked. "Unfortunately, Daddy dearest isn't very smart. If he were, he'd realize that the men he pissed off don't care about his life. They're eager for his death."

Lana gasped. "You're going to kill my father?" She swayed on her feet, looking close to fainting. "So this is all a trap? Make him think he's going to give himself up for me, and then kill him? Kill all of us?"

"That's about the gist of it." Le Clair gestured to the white van, then nodded to Kilo and Oscar. "Get our passengers settled, boys."

Deacon stiffened as Kilo dragged him toward the van. This "exchange"…it was simply another word for bloodbath. They would all be slaughtered—Hank Kelley, his daughter, Deacon himself. His own death didn't bother him. It was Lana's. The thought of watching her die sent pulses of rage to his blood. It spread, heating his insides, squeezing his heart, until he could barely see straight.

No way. There was no damn way he would let Lana be killed.

As they neared the back of the van, Deacon took a breath, set his jaw and whirled around. He launched himself at Kilo, barreling into the bigger man with such force they both went crashing to the ground. Despite his bound wrists, he landed a hit to Kilo's jaw, hard enough to split the man's lip. Blood spurted from the corner of Kilo's mouth. He spat it out, dark eyes blazing with ire. Before Deacon could blink, he was on his back with Kilo's fist in his gut.

"Enough with the games." Irritation tinged Le Clair's words. "Give it up, Delta. You're not going anywhere."

After one last punch into Deacon's side, Kilo wiped the blood from his mouth and angrily hauled Deacon to his feet. "Get in the van," he snapped.

Holding his fastened wrists against his belly, Deacon managed a resigned nod, then climbed into the back of the van. A pair of panicked blue eyes greeted him.

"What the hell are you doing?" Lana barked as the doors slammed shut with a loud thud, bathing them in darkness. "What *was* that, Deacon? They could've killed you."

"They're going to kill me anyway," he said grimly. Slowly, he lifted his hands. "It was the only way I could get this."

Lana's eyes widened as a bluish light illuminated the darkness. It was the screen of Kilo's cell phone, which Deacon had swiped from the man's pocket when he lunged at him.

"We have to call my dad to warn him," she whispered.

Deacon shook his head. "His phone will be tapped," he reminded her, already dialing a number.

"Who are you calling then?"

"An old contact at the Bureau." When the switchboard operator of the Hoover building came on the line, Deacon lowered his voice and said, "I need the extension for Colin Reilly."

He waited, stifling a groan when a few beats of elevator music met his ears. Reilly didn't keep him waiting for long, though. Several moments later, a familiar Boston accent barked out a greeting.

"Reilly, it's Deacon Holt. Listen carefully, because I don't have a lot of time here."

A wary pause. "Holt?"

"Yes." Impatience rose inside of him. "I need you to get a message to someone. It's a matter of life and death. I've got Lana Kelley here with me."

Reilly let out a shocked breath. "Are you messing with me, Holt?"

"I'm assuming you've heard about her disappearance then."

"It's all over the news."

"Does the Bureau have agents on the case?"

Reilly hesitated. "You know I can't divulge that."

Damn bureaucrats. That meant yes then.

"Listen to me, Reilly. She's here with me. We've been captured by Paul Le Clair, I know you've heard of him." The cell phone let out three mechanical dings. Low battery. Deacon cursed softly. "Look, you need to get in touch with the agents in charge of the Kelley abduction. Tell Hank Kelley the exchange is a trap. He can't show up alone, you understand, Reilly?" Three more warning chimes sounded, prompting Deacon to talk faster. "Le Clair has no intention of letting Kelley or his daughter get out of this alive. You need to make sure that—"

The connection died. Cursing again, Deacon dropped the useless phone on the floor of the van and kicked it underneath Lana's seat.

"Do you think he'll believe you?" Lana asked, urgency thickening her voice. "Will he warn them?"

Deacon took a long breath, then released it slowly. "I sure as hell hope so."

"You're not going alone," Jim Kelley insisted for the hundredth time, fixing yet another steely gaze on his father.

Hank's jaw was set in a stubborn line. "I already told you, boy. I'm not about to play games with my daughter's life. The man said to come alone."

Jim fought a wave of sheer frustration. He glanced around the massive room at his twin brothers, seeing the same frustration on their faces. Dylan had flown in from L.A. the moment the kidnappers had called to arrange the exchange. He'd wholeheartedly agreed with Jim's assessment that their father was taking an unfathomable chance here, as did Cole and Gage, who'd been trying to talk Hank out of it for hours now. Lowe and Hartman, the two federal agents sitting on the couch opposite Hank, had also tried discouraging the senator, but to no avail.

Hank was determined to do this on his own. Atonement, Jim knew. For the first time in his sorry life, Hank Kelley was trying to clean up his own mess.

And what a mess it was.

From what Jim understood, his father had gotten mixed up with a secret society whose main goal was to assassinate President Joe Colton. Freaking figured. His dad couldn't just stick to cheating on his wife, could he? No, he had to involve himself in *presidential assassinations.* Aim high, that had always been Hank's motto.

Jim had sat there in disbelief when Hank confessed everything. Apparently, after he learned of the assassination plot, Hank had tried to extricate himself from the situation, but the men he'd joined up with had panicked. Hank Kelley knew too much and, therefore, needed to be eliminated. Everything that had ensued, Lana's kidnapping, the sabotage on Cole's ranch, the attack on Hank in town—it was all done to lure Jim's father out of hiding.

And it had worked. Hank had decided to sacrifice himself for Lana, no matter how foolhardy this plan was.

"Hank."

Jim's head lifted at the sound of his mother's quiet but commanding voice. She was still in Martha's Vineyard being watched like a hawk by the guard Jim assigned to her, but she refused to be kept in the dark, and had demanded to be included in any discussion. She'd been on speakerphone this entire time, and like the others, Sarah sounded increasingly upset by her husband's decision to handle the exchange alone.

"You can't do this by yourself." Sarah's tone softened. "I know you want to bring Lana home, but you'll be risking both of your lives if you don't let the boys or the FBI help you."

Jim heard a cell phone vibrate, noticing from the corner of his eye as Special Agent Lowe rose from the sofa to take a call.

"I won't allow anyone else to get hurt," Hank told his wife. "I'm responsible for everything that's happened. I need to be the one to fix it."

"Not at our daughter's expense," Sarah shot back. "The FBI is trained to handle kidnappings. You, Hank Kelley, are not."

Jim only half listened as his parents argued, far more interested in the hushed conversation Agent Lowe was conducting across the room. The man's broad shoulders had stiffened, his brow furrowed as he listened. Something was up. The agent's body language convinced Jim of it.

He was right. A few seconds later, Lowe stalked over and rested both hands on the arm of the sofa. "There's been a development," Lowe announced, cutting Sarah off in mid sentence.

The room fell quiet.

"A call just came through headquarters' main switchboard from a man claiming to be with your daughter." Lowe studied Hank's face. "His name is Deacon Holt. Are you acquainted with him?"

Hank was quick to shake his head. "Never heard of him."

"Well, he claims he's with Lana, and he had a warning for us." Lowe's jaw tensed. "He says the exchange is a trap. The kidnappers plan to kill you on sight."

Hank wheezed out a breath. "And Lana?"

"She's going to be killed, too."

This time, the silence that descended on the room was thick with tension.

"Okay." Hank's Adam's apple bobbed fervently as he swallowed. "Okay. What do we do?"

Jim spoke up. "We come up with a new plan. One that doesn't include arranging a funeral for Lana, or damn it, you. Sound good?"

Hank nodded in resignation.

Chapter 16

When the van came to a stop three hours later, the slam of the brakes nearly sent Lana flying off the bench. She steadied herself and shot a rueful look at Deacon. "This is it."

He met her gaze. "Yes it is."

Car doors slammed, followed by the sound of footsteps. A tremor of fear dashed up her spine. Lana lowered her hands to her belly, covering the small bump protectively. Deacon didn't miss the gesture.

"I won't let them hurt you," he said quietly.

She sighed. "I don't think there's anything you can do to stop it. Not this time."

Pure helplessness exploded in his eyes. When he looked at her like that, she almost believed he might love her. That the heartless words he'd hurled her way last night had been nothing but a last-ditch attempt to avoid his true feelings. But she knew better. Deacon wasn't one to mince words. They'd spent two months together, long enough for her to get to know him, to grasp that he said what he meant, even if it wasn't something the other person wanted to hear.

He didn't love her. But at least she got comfort from the knowledge that he would do everything in his power to protect her and their baby.

"When this thing goes down, I want you to stick close to me," Deacon said. "Don't move an inch unless I tell you, okay?"

Swallowing, she nodded. "Okay."

Footsteps approached the doors, which were thrown open. Lana blinked from the sudden flood of light. Kilo's large body loomed in front of them. His nose was caked with dried blood, and the expression on his face revealed the anger he still felt over Deacon besting him.

"Get out," he ordered.

Lana exchanged a look with Deacon. He gave a small nod.

She climbed out of the van and immediately examined her surroundings. They were in an abandoned industrial area, judging from the crumbling brick buildings and random pieces of machinery scattered on the gravel. A long line of storage units stretched out to her right, but many of the doors gaped open, revealing dark empty spaces. There was some metal scaffolding to the left, broken and rusty, and then a whole lot of nothing. Just a paved lot that ended after a hundred yards or so, and a field with yellowing grass and a sagging chain-link fence.

Lana turned as Deacon hopped out of the van, his bound hands clasped to his stomach. Like her, he did a thorough sweep of the area. His lips thinned, as if he weren't happy with what he saw.

Le Clair stalked up, cell phone in hand. "Any minute now," he said with a smile. He glanced at his men. "Make sure we're secure."

The men headed off, weapons drawn, in the direction of the deserted buildings. One by one, voices crackled from Le Clair's radio to declare, "Clear." Lana recognized each voice, noticing that Echo had yet to report in. She'd seen him creep around to one of the farther storage units.

Le Clair frowned, clicked on the radio. "Echo, check in," he barked.

A moment of static, then, "Clear."

Le Clair's features relaxed. He ordered Echo and Tango to station themselves by the buildings, then barked for Kilo and Oscar to return to the vehicles.

Tension gathered in Lana's body. Le Clair's hawklike gaze scanned the area, focusing more than once on the pebble-littered road they'd driven in on. He was on guard. Impatient.

Her father would be coming from that direction. And if Deacon's warning to the FBI had gone unheeded, there was a great chance her dad wouldn't be leaving here alive.

Seconds ticked by painfully slowly. Le Clair glanced at his watch. Kilo and Oscar were ready with the rifles.

A minute passed. Two. Three. Lana's ears perked as the distant hum of a car engine broke through the cold afternoon air. She craned her neck, peered at the gravel road, gasping when the front bumper of a beige Mercedes came into view. She didn't recognize the car, but it was a model her father enjoyed.

Her pulse kicked up a notch.

"About time," Le Clair muttered.

The Mercedes crept closer, driving unbearably slowly. The nearer it got, the faster Lana's heart thumped in her chest. She could just make out the driver—male, salt-and-pepper head, a tailored black suit jacket.

Her father.

She swallowed down a lump of panic. He'd

come alone. Damn it! Deacon's warning had fallen on deaf ears.

The Mercedes stopped twenty yards from the van. Lana's heart was in her throat as she watched her father get out of the car. The very sight of him shocked her to the core. He looked nothing like the man she remembered, the man she'd seen only six months ago. His face was thinner, haggard and weary defeat swam in his eyes. He was in his late fifties, but suddenly seemed far older. Gaunt and broken and completely beaten.

Lana took a step, then thought better of it. Deacon's order to stay put resonated in her mind, but she wanted so badly to alert her father of her presence. Le Clair and Tango were shielding her from his view.

Le Clair nodded at Kilo. "Search him."

Slinging his rifle over his shoulder, Kilo strode to the car. As Lana watched, Kilo patted her father down with enormous hands, then proceeded to inspect the interior of the Mercedes.

She heard some muffled words. Her father bent through the open driver's window and released the trunk lever. Kilo rounded the car, lifted open the trunk and slammed it down a second later.

With a satisfied nod, Kilo rejoined the group. "He's clean. So's the car."

Le Clair glanced at Lana's father. "Walk toward us, Senator. Do it slowly."

"I'm not doing a damn thing until I see my daughter," Hank said loudly.

"As you like." With a gracious sweep of the arm, Le Clair stepped aside and gave Hank what he wanted.

Tears filled Lana's eyes the moment she met her father's gaze.

Hank stumbled, leaning against the car for support. "Lana! Baby, are you all right?" he shouted at her.

Her throat was so tight she couldn't get a word out. Instead, she nodded, while tears ran down her cheeks.

"Safe and sound, as you can see," Le Clair

said impatiently. "Now walk toward us. Hands on your head."

Hank lifted his arms and clasped his fingers together at the crown of his head. He took a step forward, as Lana battled the tears seeping from her eyes. She wanted to shout for him to turn around, drive away, save himself, but the hinge of her jaw seemed to be welded together, her teeth chattering as the fear and horror of these past two months flooded her body like water from a dam that had broken inside her.

The closer her father got, the faster her heart raced. No. She couldn't let this happen. She didn't know why Le Clair hadn't shot her dad outright, but it wouldn't be long before he did. Wouldn't be long before her father lay on the cold ground with a bullet hole between the eyes. Like Rick Garrison. Oh, God. She couldn't let that happen. She couldn't—

Chaos!

Lana barely had time to blink before the entire area erupted in commotion. Men seemed to pop out of nowhere like cardboard targets in a shooting range. They swarmed out of the buildings behind them, weapons drawn from all directions as shouts for Le Clair to surrender echoed in the deserted area.

From the corner of her eye, Lana saw Echo being dragged out of a storage unit, arms cuffed behind his back. And then an explosion of gunshots ripped through the air. Beside her, Kilo dove for cover behind the SUV, his rifle spitting out bullets that clanged against the metal scaffolding and bounced off the pavement. Tango rolled to the ground, shooting at the approaching attackers.

Lana's pulse shrieked, her ears ringing. Her feet were suddenly yanked out from under her, just as a bullet slammed into the side panel of the van, right where her head had been. Dazed, she found herself staring at the gravel, while a heavy weight pressed down on her back.

"Stay down," a voice hissed in her ear, and she realized what had happened. Deacon had thrown her to the ground. He was keeping her out of the crossfire.

A loud thud came from beside them. Kilo had fallen to the ground. She turned, saw the hole in his forehead, the lifeless expression on his face. Sick satisfaction coursed through her. He was dead.

She heard an enraged roar, and when she peered up from under Deacon's heavy arm, her body became paralyzed with panic. Le Clair was charging her father like an incensed bull looking to gore a matador. A blur of movement flashed before her eyes. Blue jackets with the letters FBI blazed across them. The glint of sunlight reflecting off the Mercedes' windshield. Le Clair's arm lifting, gun raising, aimed at her father.

"No!" Lana screamed.

She struggled to get out from the unrelenting shield of Deacon's body, but he forced her down, one strong arm pinning her by the collarbone.

"Put your weapon down!" Loud voices barked orders at Le Clair, but the man was beyond listening.

Lana couldn't see his face, but she could imagine his expression. Fury. Desperation. He'd come here to do a job, and he would finish it, no matter the cost.

She tried to peer around Deacon again. "Don't move," he ordered into her ear. "Stay down until it's over."

Another gunshot cracked in the air, followed by a second one.

Fear jammed in her chest. With a sudden jolt of strength, she shoved Deacon's arm off and rolled to the side, lifting her head just in time to see Le Clair tumble face-first to the pavement. A red stain bloomed on the back of his shirt. Relief crashed into her. Le Clair had been shot. Not her dad. Not—a crushing weight of horror nearly knocked the wind right out of her.

Her father's motionless body lay on the gravel. Nausea rose up her throat. "Dad!"

She heard Deacon's rough protest. Ignored him. Stumbled to her feet.

Waves of dizziness rolled through her as she hurried to her father. Voices shouted at her, people moved in and out of her peripheral vision. She ignored all that, too. She had one goal. One destination.

She froze when she spotted the blood pooling at her father's temple.

He'd been shot in the head.

"No," she whispered.

Her knees turned to jelly and her legs started to give out. Sirens wailed in the distance. Lights flashed from the road as a whiz of emergency vehicles raced toward them. But she couldn't rip her gaze away from that puddle of blood. Her father's face was pale. So pale. He was… She couldn't…couldn't get to him.

Black spots danced in front of her eyes, a dizzy rush made her body sway, and then a pair of strong warm arms wrapped around her from behind.

"It's all right," a familiar voice murmured. "You're safe, baby girl. I've got you."

She lifted her head, met her brother's concerned dark eyes and began to sob. "Jim! Oh, God, Jim, Daddy was hit!"

"It's okay," he soothed, stroking her hair. "They're going to take care of him."

Lana suddenly registered the sound of urgent voices and hurried footsteps. She turned in time to see a pair of paramedics bending over her father's body. A third rolled a stretcher over.

"We've got a pulse," she heard one of them say, triumphant.

Relief shuddered through her. He was alive. Her father was alive.

Burying her face against her brother's chest, she continued to cry softly. Jim just held her, touching her hair, whispering, "It's okay," over and over again. Her tears stained the front of his shirt, her cold hands, still in restraints, clung to his neck. A myriad of emotions swirled inside her. She'd almost lost her dad. Almost lost her own life. Her baby's life.

The baby.

Deacon!

She jerked out of Jim's arms, her gaze darting anxiously around the crowded area. Where was he? He wasn't by the van, where he'd shielded her from harm. Her head swiveled, eyes searched, heart thumped wildly.

And then she saw him. Two federal agents were shoving him into a black car. A flash of silver caught her eye. Handcuffs. Deacon was being arrested.

Ignoring Jim's shocked expression, she staggered forward, trying to get to Deacon, but he was already inside the car. Doors slammed. An engine roared to life.

"No!" she shouted when the taillights blinked and the car began to move.

Jim's hand clamped down on her shoulder. "What the hell are you doing?" he demanded.

The car sped past them. Lana caught a glimpse

of Deacon's face in the back window. He looked stoic, sad, and then she could no longer see him.

She spun around to face her brother. "You can't let them arrest him!"

Jim frowned. "Who?"

"Deacon Holt. He saved me." Her voice held a note of urgency. "They have to let him go, Jim! I'd be dead if it weren't for him."

The frown curling her brother's mouth deepened. "What exactly is he to you, Lana?"

A dozen lies sprang to her lips. She could say Deacon was an undercover cop. A kidnapper who'd defected. A friend. A total stranger.

She took a breath, opened her mouth and what came out was, "He's the father of my baby."

The waiting room of Helena General Hospital was packed to the gills with Kelleys. Lana couldn't remember the last time her entire family was gathered in one small space like this. Cole, Dylan, Jim. Her mom, Uncle Donald, his wife Bonnie Gene. Along with the family, several others occupied the uncomfortable plastic chairs. Cindy and Bethany, the twins' respective loves. Hank's bodyguard, Gage, and his girlfriend, Kate. Even Lana's best friend, Caitlin, had come to the hospital, despite the fact that she'd apparently gone through an ordeal of her own just recently.

Lana only managed a brief smile in Caitlin's direction. She would speak her to later, after the adrenaline pulsing in her blood dissipated. After she was able to take a breath without her entire chest squeezing with pain and regret. Deacon had been arrested. No matter how up in the air things were between them, she felt that she'd failed him. She'd promised she would make sure he escaped punishment, and instead, she'd stood by and watched him being driven away in handcuffs.

It didn't help that her brothers kept shooting cloudy and suspicious looks in her direction. Her confession to Jim had been passed along to everyone in the waiting room by now, and more than once she'd noticed her uncle Donald glancing at her tummy. None of them approved of, or even understood, this pregnancy, and the disappointment emanating from the mob of bodies in the room had been so unbearable she'd had to leave.

Now she sat in a smaller waiting room near the nurses' station, which she'd discovered after pretending she needed to use the restroom. It was nice to be alone. Her father was still in surgery, would probably be there for several more hours, and the last thing she wanted to do was face her family's questions and displeased faces.

"There you are."

Lana lifted her head as her mother entered the room. With her long blond hair, porcelain skin and eyes the same shade of blue as Lana's, Sarah looked more like her older sister than her mother. Only the faint wrinkles around her eyes and mouth revealed her age.

Suppressing a sigh, Lana watched her mom approach, searching the familiar face for any hint of reproach or accusation. But her mother's expression radiated softness and warmth and deep compassion.

"May I join you?" Sarah asked quietly.

Lana managed a nod.

The second Sarah settled into the chair next to hers, she wrapped a protective arm around Lana's shoulder and pulled her close. "I'm so happy you're safe, honey. I was going out of my mind the past couple months."

Lana looked over to see tears glistening in her mother's eyes. She immediately took her hand and clasped it tightly. "I'm all right, Mom. They didn't hurt me."

Sarah's gaze dropped to Lana's belly.

"It wasn't like that," she said quickly. "It happened before I was taken."

"Jim said that you told him he saved you… the father of your baby."

She nodded. "Deacon helped me escape. He was bringing me back to Maple Cove when Le Clair and his men found us."

"Then I owe him a great debt. He brought my baby home to me."

Tears prickled behind Lana's eyelids. "The FBI arrested him. I didn't have time to clear everything up. It all happened so fast, and then... he was gone."

Sarah rubbed her shoulders in a familiar maternal gesture. "Tell me about him. This Deacon."

God, where did she even start? She could see the questions swimming in her mother's eyes, but she had no idea how to answer them.

Sensing Lana's dismay, Sarah chuckled. "How about we start with an easy one?" She paused. "Do you love him?"

Chapter 17

Lana burst out laughing. "You call that easy?" Leave it to her mother to ask the one thing she'd been agonizing over for weeks now.

"Well, do you?" Sarah prodded gently.

She bit her lip, letting the question settle. "Yes," she confessed. "But he doesn't love me."

Before she could stop it, a stream of words rushed out of her mouth. She told her mother everything. The night at the Louvre. The men on the train. The horrifying discovery that Deacon was involved in her abduction. Their time on the run. His final declaration to her.

When she finished, her heart was beating wildly, and her palms went damp as she voiced one last thought. "We don't have a future, Mom."

Sarah smoothed the top of Lana's head. "Why do you say that?"

"Well, for one, he's not interested. He says he doesn't want to be a father or a husband. He thinks I deserve better than him."

"And what do *you* think?"

"I don't even know anymore," Lana burst out in frustration. "From the start, I saw something decent in him. I was convinced that deep down he was a good man. But then he shut down on me. He said some really hurtful things, too. And…and he *was* involved in my kidnapping! I know he redeemed himself in the end, but maybe he was right all along when he kept telling me he wasn't a good person."

Her mother fell silent for a long moment, then shifted in her chair so they were face to face. "Oh, honey, you still don't get it, do you?"

Lana faltered. "Get what?"

"Baby, nobody is all good and all bad. We all have our dark moments, our shades of gray." Sarah sighed. "Do you think Deacon's actions saved your life?"

"I know they did."

"And are those the actions of a bad man?"

She bit her lip again. "No, but…"

"But nothing. You know, I've always worried about you," her mother admitted. "You want everything to be beautiful and perfect. You always have, even as a child, and I supposed that's admirable in many ways, but it's also unreasonable at times. Nobody is perfect, honey. You need to learn to accept the good and the bad. It's okay to seek out the best in people, but if you remain blind to their flaws, you'll only hurt yourself in the end."

"Maybe. But none of that matters." Her eyes stung. "He doesn't love me."

"Sure he does."

She had to grin at her mom's careless tone. "Oh, does he?"

Sarah began to recite facts. "He protected you from his boss. He helped you escape. And Jim said Deacon threw himself on you when the bullets started flying. That, my darling, is love."

"Or duty," she whispered. "He felt he owed me something. How do I know that's not the reason he did all of that?"

"Well, there's a simple way to find that out."

"There is?"

"Ask the man if he loves you," Sarah said with a tiny smile.

"I would, except he's in jail," she pointed out.

"But he doesn't have to stay there." Her mother's smile widened. "We're Kelleys, honey. Might as well make good use of our connections, no?"

Deacon paced the small cell, his boots wearing away at the floor. His shoulders tensed at every noise, every random creak that sounded in the holding area of the police station. It was foolish, believing someone would actually come and give him news of Hank Kelley's condition, but he was going crazy not knowing. Lana would be destroyed if her father died.

He'd actually had to use all his strength to keep her down when the gunshots had been blazing above them, and yet she'd still managed to climb out of his grip to run to her father. He'd never forget the look on her face, that steely determination to get to a person she loved.

Funnily enough, he'd felt that same determination in his own blood. The need to run after Lana and keep her safe had been as powerful and basic as the need to breathe.

He froze in front of the bars as a sudden realization dawned on him.

In that moment, with his self-preservation in jeopardy, his head in danger of meeting a bullet, he'd only been thinking about Lana.

Would his father have done that?

A harsh laugh burst from his mouth. No, he was fairly certain his dad would've used his mother's body as armor to save his own skin.

Pressure squeezed Deacon's chest. His breathing grew ragged. He'd put Lana first. He'd been doing that since the moment she was abducted from the train station.

What did that mean? Why had he done that? *Because you love her.*

He leaned his forehead against the bars, letting the metal cool his suddenly hot skin. He couldn't ignore it anymore. From the second he'd met Lana Kelley, he'd been overwhelmed with emotion. Ridiculously intense emotions. That same intensity had consumed his father and destroyed his mother, but it hadn't destroyed Lana. Even when she told him about the pregnancy, after withholding the truth for so long, he hadn't snapped.

His father would have snapped.

News flash, buddy, you're not your father.

Deacon sucked in a shock-tinged breath. Clarity sliced into him. No, he *wasn't* his father. The destiny he'd always believed lay in store for him…well, that was nothing but a load of bull.

He controlled his destiny. And he couldn't live his life waiting for the darkness in him to spill out. Couldn't avoid caring about others in fear that it would.

Damn it, he cared about Lana. He *loved* her.

Along with the liberating rush of joy that swelled in his belly came the crushing blow of frustration. He was in prison. There was nothing he could do for Lana as long as he was in here, not even tell her how he felt.

A door swung open, bringing a gust of warm air into the somewhat cool holding area. Footsteps came from the end of the block, growing louder and heavier, until one of the FBI agents who'd arrested him stepped into view.

"Looks like you've got friends in high places," the agent announced with a reluctant look.

A uniformed officer approached from behind, already unclipping the key ring from his black leather belt. Deacon fought a spark of hope. No, this couldn't be happening. Not even Lana had the kind of power to save him from the kidnapping charges hanging over his head.

Did she?

His hope deepened when the officer stuck a key into the cell door and pulled it open.

Deacon didn't move. "What's going on?" he asked warily.

"You're free to go," the federal agent said with a shrug. "There's a car waiting outside to take you to Helena General."

Deacon just stood there, thunderstruck.

"Christ, get out here," the agent grumbled. "I'm not about to keep the Kelleys waiting."

With legs heavier than lead, Deacon walked out of the cell. Lana had kept her promise. She'd actually saved his ass.

For a moment, he contemplated ordering the car to take him to the airport instead of the hospital. He could disappear. Empty out his bank account, fly to an island somewhere and live his life the way he'd always planned—alone.

But the thought disappeared as quickly as it

had appeared. Squaring his shoulders, he followed the agent out of the holding area, a smile lifting the corner of his mouth.

Screw living alone.

He'd much rather claim the love of his life and spend the rest of his life doing everything humanly possible to make her happy.

Lana changed out of the blue hospital gown the doctor had forced her to put on, quickly changing into a pair of clean jeans and the baggy green sweater her mom had thoughtfully brought for her. She slipped her stockinged feet into comfortable brown loafers, then tied her hair in a loose twist atop her head.

The doctor had given her a clean bill of health after forcing her to endure an uncomfortable pelvic exam and an awe-inspiring ultrasound. The baby was fine. She was fine.

Her father, however, was not.

She sat back down on the gurney, impatience rising inside her. The doctor had left the room to get her some prenatal vitamins, but she didn't want to sit here and wait. Twenty minutes ago, the surgeon who'd operated on her dad had informed the family that Hank was in a medically induced coma. Although the bullet that had entered his temple had fortunately avoided damaging her father's brain, the swelling had been impossible to manage. If it continued to swell, the doctors feared it would result in brain damage, and Lana's mother promptly signed the consent form allowing them to induce a coma in order to control the swelling.

Lana was eager to see her dad, even though she knew he probably wouldn't even know she was there. Despite the choices he'd made that had contributed to her abduction, she wanted to be there for him.

The door swung open, and she hopped off the gurney, ready to snatch those vitamins from the doctor's hands and head back up to ICU.

But it wasn't the doctor who stood in the doorway.

Her heart flipped as her gaze collided with Deacon's. He still wore the faded jeans and black sweater he'd had on earlier, and she noticed specks of gravel stuck in his close-cropped hair. But other than that, he looked unharmed.

"He did it," she breathed.

Deacon moved closer, his hazel eyes flickering with confusion. "Who did what?"

"My uncle Donald. I asked him to help get you out of jail."

"Well, he succeeded."

They stared at each other for a few long moments. Lana wanted to hurl herself into his arms, but she forced her feet to stay rooted to the tiled floor. She knew he'd only come here to thank her. Maybe even to say goodbye.

Just because she'd helped set him free didn't mean he would bow down in front of her and profess his undying love.

Deacon gestured to her belly. "Did the doctor check you out?"

She nodded. "The baby and I are both fine."

Relief flashed across his face. "Good."

Another silence descended.

"Deacon—"

"Lana—"

She stopped, a fleeting smile crossing her mouth. "You first."

"I…" He trailed off, his chest rising as he took a deep breath.

And then he swiftly moved toward her and she found herself enveloped by his strong arms. His heartbeat hammered against her chest, his warmth surrounded her, his lips grazed the top of her head. "God, Lana, I'm so glad this is all over. I don't know what I would've done if you'd been hurt."

She pressed her face in the crook of his neck, breathing in his familiar scent, spicy and masculine and unbearably heady. The goodbye would come soon. She knew it. But she couldn't bring herself to break free of the embrace. She felt so small and fragile in his arms. Safe. Happy. She didn't want the feeling to go away just yet.

"There's something I need to say to you."

Disappointment flattened down on her chest. Slowly, she stepped out of his arms, forcing an indifferent look on to her face. Here it came.

"I know what you're going to say," she murmured, averting her eyes. "So don't bother. I get it, everything you said in the motel room holds true. You don't want me or this ba—"

"I love you," he interrupted.

Her head jerked up. "What?"

"I love you," he repeated, his voice thick with emotion she'd never dreamed she'd hear from him. "So much, sweetheart. And everything I said at the motel—" He laughed harshly. "It was a damned lie."

Was she hearing things?

"When I first took the job Le Clair offered, I was in it for the money," he admitted. "And then I met you, and suddenly the money didn't seem so important anymore. These last two months, the only thing I've wanted, the only thing I cared about, was keeping you safe."

Raw emotion sliced his rough features as he continued. "I figured it was duty, a way to redeem myself, but when I was in that jail cell, I realized I did all that because of *you*. Because I'm madly in love with you."

He looked so surprised by his own words she couldn't help but laugh. Then a thought occurred to her. "Are you sure you're not just saying all of this because you feel you owe me for getting you out of jail?"

"Oh, I owe you," he agreed, giving her a rare grin. "But not only because of that. You did the impossible, sweetheart. You made me want to live again. You made me see there's a light at the end of that dark tunnel, a future within my grasp, if I just quit being afraid to grab on to it."

Her heart skipped a beat.

"I want to be a different man, Lana. A *better* one." His voice cracked endearingly. "And I want to be with you, if you'll still have me."

The word *yes* nearly flew out of her mouth, until a dark thought crept into her brain. "You won't get only me," she whispered, her hands sliding down to her tummy.

To her astonishment, Deacon covered her hands with his own, wonder seeping into his gaze as he felt the bump at her waist. "I want you both," he whispered back.

"You do?"

He stroked her stomach in the most gentle of caresses. "This child is a miracle. I never wanted to be a father before I met you, but now… I want to take care of you. Both of you." A smile lit up his face. "Our son or daughter is never going to want for anything. I'll make sure of that."

"Love," she said softly. "That's all he or she needs. That's all I need, Deacon."

He slid his hands up her body, grazing her breasts, touching her neck, then cupped her chin between his warm palms. "Then that's what you'll get."

She leaned into his touch, basking in his tenderness, the softness of his normally hard features. "I love you, Deacon." She stood on her tiptoes and brushed her lips over his. "We both love you."

Uncertainty flickered in his gorgeous hazel eyes. "What about your family?"

"They're going to love you, too." She grinned. "My mom is already trying to think of ways to repay you for saving my life. And my brothers, well, they'll come around eventually."

Deacon looked doubtful. "Come around? To the fact that their little sister is marrying the mercenary who kidnapped her? Make that, unemployed mercenary."

His brief sentences contained so much startling information she didn't even know which tidbit to focus on first. She finally chose the one that made her heart soar like a hot air balloon.

"Marrying?" she teased. "Who says I'm marrying you?"

He exuded a surprising glimmer of arrogance. "Our kid can't be born out of wedlock, sweetheart."

"Oh, so now you're Mr. Traditional?"

"Hell, yes." His lips dropped to her mouth in a quick little kiss. "Are you rejecting my proposal?"

She pretended to mull it over. "I guess not."

"That's what I thought."

He bent his head again, and this time, when he kissed her, neither one of them came up for air for a very, very long time.

Epilogue

As much as it pained him to admit it, Jim had never seen his little sister look happier. Her cheeks were a rosy pink as she beamed up at the tall, muscular man at her side, whose hand she hadn't let go of since the second they'd entered the waiting room. It also pained him to notice the stark emotion and overwhelming love on Deacon Holt's face. The man loved his sister. There was no denying that.

Jim couldn't help but glance at his sister's stomach, still floored by the notion that there was a baby inside there. Lana was going to be a mother. Christ. And marrying Deacon Holt, to boot.

Despite his reservations, particularly since his future brother-in-law had played a part in Lana's abduction, Jim found himself unable to voice any disapproval. No one else in the room had the heart to do it, either. Lana looked so incredibly contented. Seemed as if there was nothing else to do but offer congratulations to the happy couple.

"Jimmy," came his uncle's low voice. "We need to talk."

With a nod, Jim followed Donald out of the room. The two men stood in the hall, where the fluorescent lighting emphasized the glint of resolve in Donald's eyes.

"What's this about?" Jim asked, though he knew full well.

"Justice." His uncle's lips tightened. "I assume you'll be on board?"

"You know I will."

"Good."

Both men glanced in the direction of the waiting room, growing quiet for a moment to listen to the happy chatter drifting from the doorway.

"I won't let these people go unpunished," Donald hissed out. "We need to find the people who hired those men to kidnap our girl. The bastards who nearly killed my brother, your father. This damn secret society that seems determined to destroy this family."

Jim had nothing to add. He was in wholehearted agreement. "I'll find them," he vowed.

"Good," Donald said again. "And I also assume we're on the same page about what to do when we find these sons of bitches?"

Lethal fury clawed up Jim's spine. "Oh, yes. When we find them, we're going to take each and every one of them down. I won't rest until every last one of those bastards is behind bars." The grin that sprang to his mouth lacked any semblance of humor. "These people are going to regret the day they decided to mess with the Kelleys."

* * * * *

Discover Pure Reading Pleasure with

Visit the Mills & Boon website for all the latest in romance

🌹 **Buy** all the latest releases, backlist and eBooks

🌹 **Find out** more about our authors and their books

🌹 **Join** our community and chat to authors and other readers

🌹 **Free** online reads from your favourite authors

🌹 **Win** with our fantastic online competitions

🌹 **Sign** up for our free monthly eNewsletter

🌹 **Tell us** what you think by signing up to our reader panel

🌹 **Rate** and review books with our star system

www.millsandboon.co.uk

 Follow us at twitter.com/millsandboonuk

 Become a fan at facebook.com/romancehq